All Bite

April Gladdis, Dog Walker Mysteries

#1

Alexa Windsor

2014

Cover Art by Rory Larsen

To Jim, Cheryl, Annie,
and Charlie,
 lots of love,

 [signature]

Chapter 1

The blond terrier I had been hired to walk would not leave that damn dead squirrel alone. She had memorized the exact path to take us by the tree where the body lay in between the roots. No matter how much I tugged at the leash in the opposite direction, Stella planted her paws into the ground. If she had the choice, she would spend the rest of the day sniffing that squirrel. Maybe she would even roll in it. Ugh.

It was the hottest part of the day. My feet ached from the five other dogs I had already walked. I was sweating underneath my camisole and I really didn't want to see gross roadkill. I shoved my hand into the pocket of my cargo shorts, hoping that I had a spare treat. I usually grabbed a handful at each house I visited. Sometimes, if I wasn't careful and threw my shorts into the laundry without remembering the treats, I would find dog biscuit residue lining the bottom of the washing machine after the cycle was finished.

Luckily, there was a single milk bone hidden in the corner of my pocket. I pried it out and leaned down, waving the small biscuit tantalizingly beside Stella's face. She stopped pulling against the leash and opened her jaws as she reached towards my hand. I snatched it away and held the treat in the opposite direction, hoping to lure her away from the route to the squirrel. At first, Stella took the bait and pursued it for a few feet, her eyes fixated on my hand, but then she remembered the real prize that awaited her by the tree and tried to go back.

"Come on, girl," I said, trying to sound cheerful. "You don't want that squirrel. Chew on that and you'll get salmonella! Or diarrhea. You don't want that, do you?"

Stella looked up at me from underneath the long hairs that made up her 'eyebrows.' I could practically hear her little doggy thoughts warring with each other. Treat. Squirrel. Big human with rope. Big meanie who won't let me get to the thing with the funky smell.

I waved the treat in front of her nose and she finally followed me again. When we got to the nearest driveway, I cupped my hand around the treat and held it out to her. She snapped it up and chewed on it between two rows of carefully brushed teeth. If her parents only knew how much she loved gnawing every tempting Styrofoam coffee cup and abandoned pizza box along the road, they would have been mortified. And even worse, I probably would have been the one they blamed.

I scratched behind Stella's ears. Something had

worked. She was willing to keep walking up the sidewalk with me until we were back in front of the large, white door of her house. There were floor-to-ceiling windows on either side of the door and acres of manicured lawn behind the house. People who could afford to live in a place like this in the middle of a Chicago suburb were some of the few who could afford to hire a daily dog walker. This family in particular had given the company I worked for business for about five years. The tips they gave me weren't too shabby, either.

    I fished around in the huge pockets of my shorts for the key ring that held my clients' house keys and unlocked the front door. Stella trotted inside and waited for me to unhook her leash before making a bee-line for her water bowl, which had been chilled with ice cubes before our walk.

    I straightened up and hung the leash up on its hook before opening a cherry-colored notebook placed on the kitchen table. Notebooks like this one were specifically for my clients and me to communicate when they weren't home. I usually jotted down the date, the time I had arrived, and any interesting or funny things that had happened during the walk. Ever since Stella caught the scent of the squirrel, I had tried to cover up that particular morbid tidbit with 'Lots of sniffing around! It's like she's looking for buried treasure!'

    I finished my note and petted Stella for a bit. Her tail wagged as she watched me leave. All of my midday walks were finished. Usually, if clients needed me to walk their dogs around noon, it was because they were at work.

They would be back in the evening to take care of dinner and take their pets out in the evening. My last visit of the day wasn't until 7:30 that evening. I would be visiting an elderly man named James Foster. I didn't know Foster's exact age, but I would guess it was in the mid-70's. He had developed an arthritis that often made walking around painful, which was the reason he needed a dog walker. For the last few weeks, I had been walking his dog, a speckled white German shorthaired pointer named Jesse, in the evening when Foster didn't have the strength to do it himself.

    I still had about five hours until that visit, enough time to go home and have dinner. I drove for ten minutes until I got to my apartment in Roger's Park. The building was made from tanned bricks and positioned at the end of a long line of cookie-cutter buildings. Sometimes the landlords would spruce up the courtyards with trees, flower bushes, and the occasional cherub-fountain like mine had. Once I got inside, my front door was up three flights of creaky stairs.

    Luckily, my apartment was affordable on a dog walker's salary with some help from my parents if things got tight. I had always dreamed of working as a veterinarian in the city. Living in Chicago had seemed like a huge adventure to a teenage girl living with her parents in small-town Illinois. I went to college for a bachelor's degree in Animal and Veterinary Sciences and found out that actually becoming a certified vet took many more years and a lot more money than I had.

    I didn't want to completely give up on my dream,

though. My town didn't offer many job prospects that would let me work with animals, so I broadened my search and found an online ad for a dog walking company called Best Furry Friends (BFF) in the northern neighborhoods of Chicago. I jumped at the opportunity. They were happy to accept me with my degree. After that, I had looked around for a relatively cheap apartment and had the great luck of finding one near where most of my clients were located.

  I had been working for Best Furry Friends for about five months. My boss, Cheryl Yin, helped me adjust to the city as best she could. Unfortunately, the first week I worked for them turned out to be the Week from Hell. During that time, my car was towed, my phone was stolen on the train, and I had my first run-in with a bunch of jerks who wouldn't stop following me until I had to duck into a nearby police station and call a cab because I was too nervous to take a bus. To top it all off, I somehow managed to lose a client's keys. I blamed the stress. I had been tired and exasperated, apologizing a million times to Cheryl and the client, who didn't want our services any longer.

  I think Cheryl just felt sorry for me at that point. She told me that the company would deal with the situation on their end. They just expected me to learn from the incident and move on. It was then I realized that I really, really liked Cheryl. She was one of the few reasons I hadn't given up on the city and moved back home with my parents. Fortunately, things managed to settle down after that chaotic week and I grew to love walking dogs and pet sitting. It let me have plenty of interaction with dogs and cats and I didn't have to deal with as much depressing sickness or injury as I would have as a vet.

As an added plus, my schedule was reasonable enough that I could take a break in the late afternoon like today. As soon as the key jiggled in the lock, my neighbor's door flew open and out popped Jennifer. She was staring at me with a manic expression underneath bouncing blonde curls.

"April! I need your help again. There's a huge bug in there!" she said. Her voice was shrill and panicked.

Jennifer and I had become friends over the past few months, bonding over the mutual experience of coming to the city and learning how to fend for ourselves. Jennifer had lived on her own for four years and got by with working two jobs – one with a theater group downtown and another as a part-time server at a little corner café on Sheridan, a major street that ran close to the Lake.

Jennifer and I helped each other out. Once I dropped my keys between the trip from my car to the apartment and she helped me scour the sidewalk until we found them. Sometimes if she got off work late at night and didn't feel comfortable taking the train back home, I would pick her up in my car. She had a car but didn't want to deal with driving it around in the downtown area if she didn't have to. It was too hard finding a place to park and the available lots charged exorbitantly for one shift. She also had the worst phobia of bugs out of anyone else I ever met. When I saw how tightly she was gripping the hem of her sweater, I knew this one was going to be big.

"How many legs does it have and where is it?" I asked.

She shuddered and she tugged on her sweater as if she could pull it down to protect her legs. "I didn't count but it looked like hundreds!"

"A silverfish?" I asked.

Jennifer frantically nodded and stepped aside so I could enter her apartment. My tennis shoes felt like the soles were caked with mud. I would feel guilty about tracking it all over her plush, beige rug, so I kicked them off and left them outside the door. I didn't worry about dirtying my hardwood floors unless they were streaked enough to warrant pulling out a mop. The rug felt wonderful underneath my aching arches.

"Did you get new sofas?" I asked, taking a box of tissues from a side table.

Jennifer beamed, admiring the brown, leather couches underneath the windows along one wall. "Yeah. I found them in a great sale yesterday. But I think I know why they were so cheap. I swear that...thing hid inside one."

I padded over to the couches, tugging a couple of tissues out of the box. It was going to be difficult catching the silverfish if it was on the carpet. I would have to try and chase it up a wall.

As though she had read my thoughts, Jennifer said, "I don't care if you don't want to kill it, just get it out of here!"

"Don't worry, I've got this. First I have to find it," I said. "Where did you last see it?"

She pointed a manicured pink nail towards the floor, just before the loveseat. "It ran underneath there."

"Help me move the couch so I can see," I said. It had been a long time since I had been to a gym. I started taking yoga classes at the beginning of summer after I first moved in and Jennifer had mentioned looking for someone to go with. I had hoped the classes would help me get stronger. Jennifer's arms were already more toned than mine. Between us, we were able to drag the leather couch across the carpet and away from the wall.

"It's in the corner! Get it, April, get it!" Jennifer exclaimed.

The silverfish was resting in the crease of the wall. What must have been fifty legs splayed out in every direction. The center pole of its body was at least two inches long. I whistled.

"Now that's a grand-daddy right there," I said, which earned me a dirty look from Jennifer. I sat on my haunches, tissues bunched in my hand, and tried to figure out how best to go about this operation. When I was eight, I had recruited myself into the silent war against the monsters of the world with more than six legs. My younger brother, Toby, and I used to hold contests to see how many bugs we could find and kill within a day. Our father used to disapprove, telling us that the bugs were minding their own business. I told him that something with that many legs was up to no good.

Since then, my feelings had mellowed out to the point where I could peacefully co-exist with bugs so long as they didn't get too close. I prided myself on being an animal person and pointed to my profession as evidence.

Now I was faced with my former enemy and I wasn't going to let it out of my sight. The silverfish's antennae swiveled as though sensing my movements. There was a pause, a breath, before I brought the wad of tissue on top of it. Jennifer gasped beside me and recoiled. I closed the tissue around it, silently praying that it wasn't going to find a way to escape and start crawling all over my arm. I rushed to the back door of her apartment, threw it open, and tossed the tissue outside. There was a small, dark blur as the silverfish slipped out if its captivity and disappeared through the cracks in the wooden staircase.

"Thank you so much! That thing was huge. I can't look at them sometimes," Jennifer said, shivering a little.

"They don't seem to realize we don't actually want them inside. The bastards," I said.

As I went to collect my shoes and go back to my apartment, Jennifer perked up a bit and said, "Hey, you're back for lunch, right? I just made some pizza pitas if you want to take a couple with you! It's my thank you for getting rid of the bug," she said.

"Actually, I might take you up on that. I love those," I said. She went off to the kitchen to fix me a plate of pitas. Her hair was still damp from a shower she must have taken before the discovery of the silverfish. The way it was frizzing caused me to run self-conscious fingers through my own honey-colored locks. My hair was nowhere near as long as hers. Mine hung down in layers to my chin, like a ruffled curtain around my head. I've been told it looks good on me, so I decided to keep the style. I didn't have the patience for the hours of hair-spray and curling-irons it took Jennifer to make her hair look like a model's dream.

"So, tell me about your dogs today? Any cute ones?" she asked as she grabbed a Tupperware container out of the cupboard.

I told her about my regular clients; a territorial German shepherd, a white Samoyed that looked like a huge cotton ball, a house with three (count 'em, three) Chocolate Labradors with the names Cocoa, Chocco, and Hershey. I didn't know many Chocolate Labs without a name based on some variety of chocolate. Maybe the owners were hungry when they named their dogs. Hopefully, no one had been on a diet.

"And then there's Jesse. I'm walking him tonight," I continued. "He's a German shorthaired pointer. Big for the breed, but he's gorgeous."

Jennifer gave me a slightly blank look before I realized that she probably had no idea what a German shorthaired pointer looked like. She hadn't been the one watching the Westminster Kennel Club's Annual Dog Show every year since she was ten. I whipped out my cell phone and did a quick Google search, pressing on the first stock photo that popped up. Pointers had been bred to be hunting and companion dogs. From what I had seen of Jesse, he fit the bill perfectly. The breed commonly had masks of a dark brown color covering their heads and faces, maybe a little splotch or two on their legs and paws as well. The rest of their bodies were white with black polka-dots. The coloring was very distinctive and on Jesse, it was gorgeous.

Jennifer's eyes lit up and she took the phone from my hand. "It's so cute! Does he do the pointing thing?" Jennifer asked. I must have looked confused, because she said, "You know, the pointing thing! They raise a paw and point with their nose." She emphasized what she said by raising her wrist, palm facing downward, and bobbing her head.

"Oh, that," I said. "I haven't seen him do it yet. Although, he does get really excited about bushes. If he points, I'll try to take a picture for you."

She handed me the plate with the pitas and I sat down at the kitchen table while she made one for herself.

"Thanks a bunch. Do you have a rehearsal tonight? Maybe we can watch a movie if you're not busy. I've still got some time before I go to my last appointment," I said.

"We're in between shows right now. I have a rehearsal tomorrow and then performances for the next three days, but I'm free tonight! What do you want to see? Oh wait, I know the answer to that," Jennifer said with a sly smile. "It wouldn't happen to be *Grimoire Danya*, would it?"

I wanted to quip back with something clever and witty, but it would have been ruined by the blush creeping up my face. "Well, maybe..."

"I knew it! You just want to stare at Rick again!" she said, giggling.

Rick Weaver was the director and writer for an online web series called *Grimoire Danya*. The show had started as a summer project by his group of friends to stave off boredom. In the beginning, it was low-budget and filmed with sub-par equipment, but that just made it charming. The series was a fantasy horror about a witch hunter in a Medieval setting who had to save the surrounding villages from monsters like banshees and ghosts. It was now three years old and had collected a dedicated fan base on the internet. Once their popularity had sky-rocketed and they could sell merchandise, they could afford better equipment and props.

My college roommate convinced me to watch it during my senior year. We spent an entire weekend playing a marathon of the episodes back-to-back. I was hooked after that, although I have to admit my obsession might have had something to do with Rick. He was twenty-four years old, had the same kind of cynical, dry humor as I did, and was a handsome and successful filmmaker. The DVDs of the web series sold by the thousands within the first few days of their release. How was a lovesick, low-income dog walker like me to resist? I had tried to convince myself that I was being silly. How could there be anything between us? For all I knew, he lived halfway across the country.

That was what I thought until I saw one of the behind-the-scenes extras on a DVD - an interview with him standing in front of the giant, Silver Bean in

Millenium Park. So, he had been to Chicago at some point, maybe even lived somewhere in the city! I started imagining what it might be like to see him walking down a random street or going into a coffee shop. Although, if he met me in person, he would probably swap one sentence with me and think I was way too awkward to hold his interest.

Oh well, a girl could dream...

I shrugged and said, "Well, what can I say? I like to enjoy the scenery once in a while." Especially if that scenery was Rick.

Jennifer refused to let the matter die. "You know, I bet if we took another good look at the show, we could figure out where he lives."

"Doesn't that seem stalkerish to you?" I said. "What would I say when I found him? 'Oh, hi Rick, fancy meeting you here in front of your house. I noticed that you seem to film in your back lawn quite a bit and I matched up your DNA with the fingerprints I found on the porch. Please go out with me.'"

"I didn't mean it like that!" Jennifer said. "I mean he probably does DVD and t-shirt signings at conventions. You could try to find him at one."

I felt warmed by the idea, but then I would just be surrounded by other fans. A face in the crowd. I would always remember shaking his hand, but he wouldn't remember me. I wanted to be more than a fan, like maybe a friend.

None of that was going to get Jennifer off my back, though. "Maybe. I'll think about it."

Jennifer grinned. "Alright. I can set things up if you want to watch it now."

Fifteen minutes later, we were both parked on her new, comfy couches with some ranch and barbecue-flavored popcorn with the DVDs of the web series on her wide screen. We would usually discuss our theories for the series, like who was going to die and what symbolized what. Once we had argued for a full hour about whether or not an apple sliced in half in one episode represented the fall of the Western Kingdoms.

Jennifer had a tendency to imagine romantic relationships in the show that the writers hadn't intended. I wouldn't have cared if she didn't go on and on about how Rick's character, Dyllas, could be paired with just about everyone (of both genders). At the mention of Dyllas getting hitched with the princess while they were riding horseback into the woods, I shoved another handful of popcorn into my mouth so that I didn't remind Jennifer that the princess was going to die in another five entries. Dyllas was married to his quest anyway, so having time for romance would be impossible!

And what if it was me on that horse with him? Would I want him to make time for romance then? I gulped down a big glass of ice water to wash down the popcorn and quell the wave of heat creeping up my neck. Luckily, Jennifer hadn't noticed.

"You know, I wonder if we could figure out a way

to get into contact with them on the internet?" Jennifer said. She whipped out her phone and brought up their Facebook pages on an app.

"That's really not necessary," I said, quickly. "I'd be too nervous to chat."

"You never know unless you try! Besides, it would get easier the more you got to know them," she said. "You know, celebrities are just people who have more money to spend on boob jobs and personal trainers."

I laughed and watched as Dyllas evaded a goblin trying to impale him on a spear. Even when he was in danger, Dyllas had a rugged charm with sandy-blond short hair and a dusting of stubble around his jaw. I'd seen pictures of him in real life and he was always clean shaven. In an interview, Rick had mentioned that he would skip shaving for a day or two before filming so he could keep his look. Whatever he did, it definitely worked for him.

Dyllas smashed the handle of his sword into the goblin's face and stole its spear. He kicked the creature and sent it reeling over a cliff. Just as he recovered and brandished his weapons to face the circle of goblins closing in around him, there was an explosion that incinerated half of the hideous group.

Part of me wondered how Rick and his team could get away with those effects without anyone calling the police on them. The explosion looked real, not just an effect made with a computer. I only had a moment to ponder this before a dashing figure carrying a sack full of bombs emerged from the smoke in silhouette on the rocks above the battlefield. This shot alone could cause a horde of fangirls to riot. The man was supposed to be Dyllas's rival, Averad, played by Mark Bishop. The pair had a love-hate relationship with both of them trying to be the first to get their hands on the magical Grimoire that the series was named after. The Grimoire was a book of magic created by the clerics of the world's god, Danya. Whoever possessed it would have powers beyond mortal comprehension. Little wonder why both of the boys would want it.

Mark had first appeared as a bit-character in the first season. Because of his good looks and witty one-liners, the fans fell in love with him and he was promoted to a script writer and given a major role.

Averad threw another bomb at the flailing goblins. Dyllas was able to slice his way through the few that were left. After he was finished, Averad leaped off the rocks and landed in front of Rick, allowing the camera to have a flattering shot centered on his face and upper body. He had dark, tousled hair and brown eyes. He had a couple of days' worth of stubble on him just like Dyllas, but Averad was a tad shorter and his skin was a light brown. He worked out quite a bit, too, by the looks of the muscles visible through his tight shirt.

I shook my head. "That is so fan service," I told Jennifer with a grin. Rick and Mark liked to throw in scenes like that every now and then just to play up the hotness of the main characters. It drew in more viewers and gave the loyal fans more reason to drool over the show.

"Well, yeah," she said. "But it works. That man is fine!"

I preferred Dyllas, personally. Maybe it was his drive for justice or his grim determination that drew me in. Maybe I just had a thing for men with hazel eyes.

Averad sauntered over to Dyllas, inspecting the charred goblin corpses with disgust.

Dyllas watched him apprehensively. "Why did you save me? You've never bothered to help me before."

"You're most welcome," Averad drawled. "And here I thought I was doing the decent thing."

"Your name and decency don't belong in the same breath," Rick said. He still hadn't lowered his weapons.

Averad tossed a bomb back and forth between his hands and chuckled. "If you must know, the lawmen that gave you the task of getting rid of these disgusting beasts gave me an offer as well."

Dyllas was taken aback. "Did they think I was incompetent?"

Averad shrugged. "It's difficult to predict who will go up against an entire horde and come back in one piece. In any case, one of us will be getting that reward and I intend for it to be me."

"Over my cold, dead body, you will," Dyllas said.

Jennifer and I said Averad's next line aloud. "That

can be arranged."

We burst out laughing as Averad unsheathed his sword and began fencing with Dyllas. That line had become Averad's trademark. You could usually predict when he would say it, which was at least once during every show.

"They probably have a quota," Jennifer said. "They know we're waiting for it."

I glanced at the clock. I had about a half hour before I had to go to Foster's apartment. I gathered my things and stood up.

"I have to get going. This was really fun," I said.

"That's right, you have a walk tonight, don't you?" Jennifer said. "Be safe out there! Don't let the puppies bite!"

Chapter 2

We said our goodbyes and I went out to my car to go back up north. Foster lived in a red brick apartment building right by the lake shore with its own private beach and gated parking lot at the side. I was envious of that parking lot. Even when it wasn't a holiday, parking on a residential street in Chicago could be a nightmare. Free spaces were coveted, more often than not.

The building was split into five floors, each connected by stairs and an elevator on the inside. The main entrance to the building had a doorman to regulate people coming in. The doorman was used to seeing me and pressed the buzzer to let me in the front door. I thanked him and took the elevator up to the fifth floor, closing my eyes during the ride and thoroughly enjoying the blasting AC. Even in the evening, the heat radiating off of concrete that had been baking in the sun all day could be brutal.

The front door to Foster's apartment was on the left of the long hall leading away from the elevator. I unlocked it with a silver key that had a custom leaf design on its handle. All of our clients had to provide us with two sets of keys when they hired the company -- one to go with the walker and the other to stay at the office in case of an emergency. Hopefully, I wouldn't do something thoughtless like lock myself out of a client's house and have to resort to using their spare set anytime soon. Accidents were bound to happen, though.

I unlocked the door and automatically reached up to disarm Mr. Foster's alarm system (he kept it on even when he was home as a precaution to protect himself and all the fancy things in his apartment, for which I couldn't blame him). A moment later, I was bombarded with Jesse's chocolate-brown face. He reared up on his hind legs and pressed forward, forcing me to hold on to his forelegs with my arms to avoid being bowled backwards. When I had said he was a big dog, I wasn't kidding. He was only a head shorter than me when he was standing up like this. I scrunched up my face and shut my mouth tightly as he drenched my face with his long tongue.

As much as I would have liked to stand there dancing with him all day, I knew Foster was trying to train Jesse not to jump on visitors. This probably wasn't setting a good precedent. I sighed and let down his front paws. He scampered towards the living room, his toenails clicking on the tiles.

"Hel-looo, it's Aaa-Pril," I called out. His hearing had gotten worse over the years, so I always tried to call out so he would know I had arrived. Didn't want to startle him too badly.

I rounded the corner to the living room, which was decorated with green, velvet-lined curtains and glass tables. In the middle of the room was a long couch with a square ottoman onto which Jesse jumped and curled up. Foster was sitting on the couch with his feet propped up next to Jesse, watching the news on a wide, flat screen television propped up on the wall. With one look at James Foster, you could tell he must have been extremely handsome when he was younger. His high cheekbones and a strong jawline were still noble, albeit smattered with wrinkles. His shoulders held a hint of being broad and straight once, but now they were hunched. His hair was gray and speckled with silver. Under the deepening lines on his forehead, his olive-green eyes had taken on a milky white hue because of the cataracts. He was dressed in a long-sleeved shirt and khaki pants and held a half-full glass of red wine in one hand.

He held up a hand in greeting when I came in. "Afternoon! I hear it's hot out there."

"Just a little bit," I said, smiling.

"Which is why I'm glad I'm in here and not out there," he said. "Would you like a glass of water or anything before you head out?"

"It's all right, but thanks anyway. I've got a water bottle in the car." I said, though I was grateful for the offering. Always nice to know the clients thought of our well-being once in a while.

Jesse had leaped off of the ottoman and grabbed a stuffed alligator in his mouth. He circled around and around the room with it.

"He's been waiting for you all afternoon. I swear he knows what days you're coming. He'll sit by the door if he sees you walking up the sidewalk through the window," Foster said.

"Well, I won't keep him waiting, then," I said. I picked up Jesse's leash from where it was slung across a hook by the door. It was a blue flat-leash with a plastic bone attached to the handle in which a roll of poop bags could be stored. A lot of clients used the bones, but a lot of them just used plastic grocery bags. I liked the convenience of the rolls because you didn't have to worry about grabbing a new bag before every walk.

Jesse was well trained not to pull on the leash or lunge at passers-by, but Foster had him walk with a harness just in case. When he saw me pick up the harness, Jesse stopped his circuit and stared up at me, his dark eyes wide and expectant. He wasn't about to put down the toy, so I worked the harness over the alligator's tail and secured the lower strap behind his front legs.

"One more thing before you leave," Foster said. He set his wine glass on a side table and stood up with a little grunt. His knees must have been giving him trouble. He was a couple inches over six feet when he was standing up straight. He definitely towered over my five-foot-four. He picked up a small, black box from the window sill and pulled out a collar. It was a simple, black band with a license-tag and a silver cylinder about the size of my thumb hanging from the tag's ring. The two jingled together when Foster came over to me and held out the collar.

"If it's not too much trouble, I'd like for him to wear this outside from now on," he said. "It's nothing to worry about, just his license and a container to hold a tracking device. I've heard about dogs disappearing, running away and such. I never expect Jesse to give you any trouble, but just in case, keep it on him. He doesn't like the sound it makes when it knocks against the tags so he doesn't like wearing it, but I'd like to get him used to it."

The request was unexpected, but understandable. I had noticed that Foster liked to take Jesse's collar off while he was home. Putting it on for walks was a good habit to develop. I took the collar from him and gently snapped it around Jesse's neck. He took it as a sign to start heading towards the door.

"Do you want me to turn on the alarm?" I asked Foster.

"No, it will be alright," he said. "I'll lock up and turn it on when you go."

"We'll be back in a bit." I let the door fall shut behind me.

As Jesse and I took the elevator to the ground floor, I couldn't help but wonder what Foster did while I was walking his dog. Maybe he just watched the news or cooked dinner. I never had the time to sit down with my clients and have a heart-to-heart talk about their personal lives. I didn't even know where most of them worked or what they did. I was there to walk their dogs or feed their cats. What else did I need to know besides how many cans of food to give Fluffy at breakfast?

    I gathered that Foster had been successful at some kind of business if he could afford to live by himself in a huge apartment right by the lake shore. Maybe he had inheritance money or he was an expert buying and selling stocks. I had seen the names of business contacts once when he had left an address book open on his counter (not that I had been snooping; I just glanced down to see it). He had small, precise handwriting, so unlike my lazy scrawling whenever I wrote notes to my clients.

    Did he have family in the city? I had never seen any pictures around his apartment of him with a spouse or with children. The only framed photos I had seen were of him by the beach with Jesse. He seemed too much like a nice old grandpa to be all by himself in the big city. Then again, he could have family somewhere else and moved away from them for some reason. I didn't know much about him at all. Maybe it was better that way.

    When the elevator stopped, Jesse squeezed his body through the doors as soon as they opened. The doorman smiled and nodded as we headed out. The sun was blinding and I immediately whipped out my shades. The humidity crawled along my skin. I really needed to install my air conditioner soon. Jennifer had already hired a couple of handymen to set up a unit in her apartment. I would have done the same if I had enough money in my pocket.

The breeze coming off of the lake made things bearable. The beach was always going to be cooler than the middle of the city. They didn't call Chicago the Windy City for nothing. What I loved about walking Jesse was how close I usually got to the beach. I had grown up surrounded by corn in central Illinois. The biggest bodies of water in that area were ponds and town reservoirs. Not exactly an ocean adventure. The lake shore in Evanston was gorgeous, with bleached sand on the beaches and manicured grass in the parks. Every so often, you could see a ferry or a yacht out on the water.

Jesse was more interested in the people walking by than the waves. I used to take him out on the public beaches before the lifeguards cracked down on the "No dogs on the beach" rule. Unfortunately, we didn't have enough time within the half-hour allotted for our walk to get to a dog beach, so we just strolled along the bike paths that ran through the nearby park.

I had noticed that strangers were sometimes a lot friendlier if you were out with a dog. One man with fiery tattoos covering his neck and arms said Jesse was a "good-looking dog" as we passed him. I thanked him and smiled. Jesse wasn't even my pet and I still glowed with pride whenever someone complimented him.

We went down a path that followed a long line of boulders that overlooked a beach. On the other side of the road, a cemetery stretched beyond my sight. There weren't as many people on this stretch, so Jesse was free from distractions as he sniffed from rock to rock. He eventually stopped to lift his leg on a nearby "NO DOGS

ALLOWED" sign. I snorted with laughter when he looked at me with an expression that said, 'What? I don't care,' before striding away.

It was about ten minutes later, with the sun beating down on me and making me wish I had brought a water bottle, when my phone rang. I glanced at the screen. I didn't like to answer calls while I was walking a dog unless my boss was calling me. To my surprise, Foster's name lit up. I had seen him not that long ago. Why was he calling me now? While Jesse sniffed at some rocks, I answered the call.

"Holding up alright, April?" Foster said, cheerfully.

"Yeah, I'm fine," I said. "What's going on?"

"The office in my building called to inform me that I have a package waiting in the front. I was wondering if you would be so kind as to pick it up for me on your way in," he said.

"Sure," I said, relieved that there wasn't a problem. "Will they let me do that?"

"I'll call down and let them know you're coming. The doorman will recognize you. Show them the key I gave you and it should be enough verification," he said. "I'm sorry, I would do it myself but my back started acting up and I want to lay down for a while."

"No, no, it's not a problem. I can get it for you," I said.

"How is Jesse doing?"

"Oh, he's uh..." I glanced at Jesse, who was nipping on a small patch of tall weeds. I held back a groan of frustration. Why did I always get the dogs that loved to munch on plants? I tugged on the leash and he raised his head. At least he was better at obeying than Stella had been with the dead squirrel. "He's just fine. I'll make sure he gets a drink of water when we get back."

"Thank you. He's a good boy, isn't he? All right, I won't keep you," Foster said.

"See you when I get back," I replied before hanging up.

Best Furry Friends didn't want the walkers to have direct contact with the clients. When I asked her why, Cheryl had told me it was a liability issue. If the client had an issue or a question, the office would handle it and then communicate with the walker if need be. The company didn't even want us swapping phone numbers if we could help it. Some of my clients had insisted that I take their number in case of an emergency. I didn't mind as long as none of them called me up while they were drunk or wanted to rant about something. That was one reason I liked the company's policy – the office handled the angry people. I didn't think I would have to worry about that with Mr. Foster, though. We had exchanged phone numbers at his request as a precaution if anything happened to Jesse. I had run it by Cheryl and she seemed to be okay with it.

The sky was just now starting to darken. I coaxed Jesse into turning around and heading back home. He peered down at the people lounging on the sand curiously.

I gently tugged on his leash so he would keep walking. We returned to the apartment building ten minutes later. My clothes were sticking to my body with sweat and I felt a bit disgusting. The first thing I would do when I got home was to get a cool shower.

    I veered off into the main office when we were inside. The lady at the desk glanced at Jesse and then smiled up at me. She had gray hairs intertwined with dry, golden ones and was wearing a pressed blouse and slacks that made me feel slightly self-conscious in my tank top and shorts. The nameplate on her desk read 'Elle Jones.'

    "Can I help you?" she said.

    "James Foster from apartment 510 wanted me to pick up a package that came for him," I said.

    "And what would your name be?" she said.

    "April Gladdis," I replied.

    "Ah, yes," she said. "He called down and told us you would be coming. May I see your ID?"

    I pulled my wallet out of my fanny pack and handed her my driver's license. She examined it briefly and handed it back.

    "Very good. Wait here and I will get the package for you." She disappeared into the room where the mail was stored and distributed into their lockers. I felt something nudge my hip and glanced down to find Jesse burying his nose in my pocket. He must have smelled the treat crumbs. I fished out a sparse handful and held out my palm. He had inhaled them by the time Elle came back.

The package was about the size of a tissue box. I took it, thanked her, and left the office to go to the elevator. Jesse stood close to me, his head resting against my thigh as we ascended to his floor. I scratched behind his ears and stroked the rich, brown fur between his eyes.

"We're almost home, boy," I told him. As soon as we were on the fifth floor, Jesse scurried ahead of me with his pink tongue lolling out of the side of his mouth. Intending to undo his harness, I released the leash when I opened Mr. Foster's front door, but he slipped inside before I could reach for him. Typical Jesse.

I closed the door, switched off the alarm, and left the package on the coffee table in the living room. The TV had been turned off so that the hum of the AC was the only thing breaking the silence. In order to get to the hall leading to the bedroom, you had to either go through the bathroom or the kitchen, which was where Jesse was currently heading to get a drink of water. I followed him in so I could take off his harness. Foster had turned off all lights when he had gone to rest, leaving the light on in the entry way for me. As soon as I turned the kitchen light back on, I gasped. There was a puddle of maroon wine and shards from a shattered glass on the floor. It looked like the same wine Foster had been drinking before I left. I called after Jesse to stop him before he stepped on the shards and hurt his paws.

It didn't seem like Mr. Foster to leave such a mess. Just when I was going to grab a towel from the bathroom to try and clean it up, I noticed that the door to the bedroom at the end of the hall was ajar. A sliver of light streamed through the gap. I guided Jesse around the broken glass and headed for the light with him close behind.

The bedroom had an ornate, Victorian throw rug upon which Foster was seated, his back propped up against the side of a queen-sized bed. He was slumped over with his legs stretched out in front of him. He looked as though he was inspecting his shirt, which he had clutched in one hand.

"Mr. Foster? Are you all right?" I asked, stepping further into the room. "I can clean up the spill in the kitchen if you want."

He didn't look up at me, even when I stood beside him. Once I had a better view of his shirt, I saw that the scrunched fabric he was holding was covered in a large crimson splotch.

"Mr. Foster?" I said, my voice sounding distant to my own ears. He wasn't moving. He did nothing to acknowledge me. My knees wobbled when I knelt beside him to get a better look at his face. His eyes were open and staring at nothing. His free arm hung limply at his side, the fingers loosely wrapped around a silver handgun.

Chapter 3

I shot to my feet and backed away.

"Mr. Foster?" I said, my voice shaking with growing panic.

This was...this was crazy. This was horrible! I had talked to him not ten minutes before! He wasn't breathing, but how could I be sure he was...dead? Should I check his pulse? No, I wasn't supposed to touch the body, right?

Jesse trotted over to his master and sniffed his hands. The moment his tongue flicked out over the blood, I grabbed his collar and tugged him away. I dragged him into the hall and closed the door. I needed to call 911 and my boss. Somebody had to help. Anybody! How the hell had this happened?!

I dug out my cell phone and dialed 911 with shaky fingers. The voice that answered was clipped.

"Evanston Emergency. Where is your location?"

It took me a second to clear the hurricane of thoughts in my head and remember Foster's address. I told it to the operator and said, "I came back from walking this guy's dog – he's my client. I came in and he was on the floor of his bedroom. He's still there. I-I don't know what happened but there's blood on his chest and he has a gun!"

"All right, Ma'am," the operator said. "Can you confirm the address before an ambulance is dispatched?" I did so in a shaky voice and he continued, "Thank you. I'm contacting the police as well. I'm going to ask you to stay on the line with me until they arrive. What's your name?"

"April Gladdis," I said. A thought suddenly occurred to me that the doorman and the main office might want to know what was going on before flashing emergency vehicles showed up on their front step. I should have thought of that before calling. I started heading towards the entryway, bringing Jesse along with me. Maybe it was a good thing that I hadn't had the opportunity to take his harness off.

"I'm going to go down to the lobby of the building I'm in and tell them an ambulance is coming," I said.

"Just stay on the line," said the operator. "Can you explain what you were doing when you found this man?"

My brain was torn in half between trying to lock the door behind me and telling the operator about finding Foster in his bedroom after the walk. Jesse was close on my heels as we went back to the elevator. The ride down to the main floor was torture. I had finished telling the operator all the details by the time I reached the front desk. The doorman stared at me, bewildered, when he saw my flushed cheeks and tear-filled eyes .

I told the operator to wait a moment while I told the doorman what was happening.

"I need to talk to the building manager. I just went to see James Foster in apartment 510 and he was..." I struggled to get the words out. "He's hurt. Badly. I called an ambulance already."

"Uh, hold on," he said before running out from behind the counter and into the main office. He emerged a moment later with a rather alarmed Elle.

"What's going on?" she asked me. I told her what I had told the doorman.

"I called 911. I'm on the line right now," I gestured to my phone.

"Let me talk to them," Elle said. I didn't think twice about handing the phone over. She spoke to the operator, but my mind was too fuzzy to listen to what she was saying. The doorman was looking between Elle and me helplessly. Finally, he turned to me.

"Are you alright? Can I get you anything?" he said.

"Do you have water?" I said. I needed a drink after the walk and this shock wasn't helping.

"Hold on, I'll check," he said. He disappeared into the office again as I sank down on one of the white couches in the middle of the lobby. I needed to call my boss, but I wouldn't be able to do it until Elle was off the phone and the emergency operator let me go. I curled my hands into fists on my lap to keep them from shaking.

By the time the doorman came back with a cup of water, I heard an approaching siren outside. Luckily, rush hour traffic lightened up around seven o'clock most evenings, so the emergency team wouldn't have to deal with it now.

Elle returned my phone and said, "He wants to ask you more questions."

I nodded and hoped I could keep my voice steady enough to answer them.

"Ms. Gladdis?"

"Yeah, I'm here."

"Was anyone else in Foster's apartment when you arrived?"

"No. I didn't see anyone else."

"Did you check any other rooms besides the ones you entered?"

"No. I didn't think about it."

"And he wasn't acting suspiciously before you came in and found him?"

"He called me and asked me to pick up a package for him while I was walking his dog. That was it," I said.

The ambulance pulled up to the curb. The operator

let me go when he was sure that the medical personnel and police were inside the lobby. A medical team had already gone up to Apt 510 with Elle after I told them Foster was in the bedroom. The moment he hung up, I dialed the number for Best Furry Friends. The operating hours for the office were closed, but they kept the line open in case the walkers had an emergency.

When Cheryl answered, I said, "I just got back from walking Jesse Foster. When we went up to see James...he was on the ground and he had blood on his shirt."

"Oh my god..." Cheryl said. Her voice shook, but she wasn't panicking. "Did he say anything to you?"

"No. He was already dead when I got there, I think," I said.

"Did you already call an ambulance?" she said.

"Yeah. They're here now. I'm in the lobby with the police.

"Are you okay?"

"Yeah, I think so," I lied.

"Just stay put, I'll be there in fifteen minutes," she said.

I said goodbye and hung up so I could face reality. This was really happening. There was a dead body four floors above my head, with blood and cold skin and everything. Said dead man had talked to me not ten minutes before I had found him. Had he shot himself?

People didn't usually shoot themselves in the chest, though. It would be too hard. Did that mean someone had attacked him? Who would want to attack a nice old man in his apartment?

There was a tap on my shoulder that startled me. I looked up to see the doorman's apologetic smile.

"I know this is a really bad time," he said, "but do you think you could keep your dog with you?"

I followed his gesture over to where Jesse was gazing out of the large windows. His nose was leaving wet smears all over the glass.

"Sorry," I mumbled before staggering over and grabbing his leash. My legs felt as though they were filled with jelly. I sat back down on the couch with Jesse meandering around me. He was panting up a storm as the doorman patted him on the head.

"I wonder what will happen to him if his owner is gone," he said.

I hadn't thought of that before. Jesse couldn't very well live by himself. If Mr. Foster didn't have any relatives in the city that could take him, would he live with someone out of town? The police would probably put him in an animal shelter until someone claimed him. The thought of him in a cage made my heart ache, but I knew the shelters in Chicago would take better care of him than that. The Humane Society would ensure Jesse was placed in a beautiful, loving home. His gorgeous face would steal anyone's heart just like it had stolen mine.

Eventually, Jesse laid down on the floor while we waited for Cheryl to arrive. An officer came up to me and took my name, age, and home address. He told me the detectives were conducting an investigation in the apartment and would want to take an initial statement from me when they were done. I was just glad that I didn't have to see Mr. Foster's body again.

There was a buzz at the front door and the doorman unlocked it to let Cheryl through. She was only a couple of inches taller than me with black hair that was pulled back into a messy ponytail. Her normally pale skin was flushed with red from the heat combined with the exercise. There were some days when she and her assistant would take the overflow work for the company. Best Furry Friends was still growing and sometimes we were too short-handed to handle the increasing number of clients. I had no idea how Cheryl was able to juggle managing the business with the extra walking.

"April? How long have you been here? Are you all right?" she said when she caught sight of me on the couch.

"I've been here since 7:30. That's when we got back from our walk," I said.

She took in the sight of the police in the lobby and the ambulance outside. "I can't believe this..."

The same officer who had spoken to me before came over. "Excuse me, ma'am, are you a resident?"

Cheryl turned to him. "My name is Cheryl Yin, I'm the owner and manager of Best Furry Friends and April's employer. I'd like to be present when she tells you her story, if that's all right."

The officer nodded. "The detectives will be down after their investigation of the scene. Please stay here until they arrive."

I tried to distract myself by petting Jesse. He was starting to get bored with watching the officers stride back and forth across the room. Cheryl crouched down next to him and he licked her face.

"Tell me what happened. Even if it's just the bare bones," she said to me. "I'll hear the rest while we're talking to the detectives."

I worried my lip before I replied, "I went up to get Jesse. Mr. Foster was fine then, but when I got back, I found him in the bedroom and he was...dead. So, I called 911 and came down here to tell the front desk."

Cheryl nodded and was quiet for a moment. "I'm sorry. That would be horrible for anyone to go through. You did well. The police will take care of everything now, don't worry."

Her words should have comforted me, but I still felt hazy inside, like I couldn't pull my mind back together after a tornado had ripped through it. There were voices echoing around the room and lights flashing outside, alternating blue and red colors across Jesse's face. Everything felt too unreal, but the blast of air conditioning on my neck reminded me that this wasn't a dream.

A pair of men wearing different suits than the other police officers emerged from the elevator. One was an older man with graying hair and a dusty mustache. A pair of thin-rimmed glasses sat over a slightly crooked nose, which looked as though it had been broken at some point in his life and hadn't healed the right way. His face was grim and slightly weary. The other man was much younger, maybe even just a few years older than my twenty-three years and had dark, slightly curly hair. He had a slender build, but I could tell he had a decent amount of muscle underneath his jacket.

After they crossed the room to meet us, the older man offered his hand in greeting. "Hello there, I am Detective Carl Winchester and this is my partner Neal Farland."

Cheryl spoke up for us both. "My name is Cheryl Yin and this is April Gladdis. I run the pet sitting company that April works for, Best Furry Friends. I'd like to be present while you are questioning her if that is possible. She was on the job when she found James Foster."

"That's fine for the initial statement. We'll decide if she needs to be brought in for further questioning later," Carl said. "First off, how are you feeling, Ms. Gladdis?"

"I'm all right...I think," I replied. I peered up at him, wondering if I looked as haggard as I felt.

"Why don't you start by telling us what happened when you first came to the building to pick up the dog and take him for a walk?" he said.

I told him everything I had told the operator on the phone earlier, trying to recall as many details as possible through the haze of shock in my mind. The walk, the phone call, coming back and finding Mr. Foster, calling 911. It all felt so surreal while I tried to describe the scene to the detectives, like all of this had happened to someone else and I was just sharing a story I had heard. All the while, I held onto Jesse's collar. Scratching behind his ears was becoming a nervous tick in the last few minutes.

After I finished, Carl said, "And you didn't see or hear anyone else inside the apartment when you returned?"

"No. I didn't think anyone else was there. I wasn't really looking," I said.

"How long would you say the first visit took?"

"Umm...a couple minutes? Not long at all, just enough to get the dog," I said.

"How long were you there when you came back?"

"Same thing, a couple minutes." I really didn't see where the detectives were going with this.

Carl rubbed at the slight scruff on his chin. "About how long after you left with the dog did Mr. Foster call you?"

"Fifteen minutes, I think. After that, it was about ten minutes before I got back to the building." It was then that I realized that Cheryl had heard me confess that I had talked to Mr. Foster directly. Hopefully she wouldn't mind in this case, even if it was against company policy. It was too late to worry about that now.

The detectives conversed quietly with each other for a moment. Something had been bothering me for a while now and I was too tired to be shy.

"Detective Winchester? Can I ask you something?" I said.

"Of course."

"Did he kill himself? I don't know if anyone can shoot themselves in the chest and he seemed so happy when I left. It doesn't make sense," I said.

Both Carl and Neal watched me very closely. Finally, Neal addressed me for the first time. "That doesn't seem plausible. We've discovered that the gun wasn't the murder weapon, first off."

Cheryl and I looked at him in surprise.

"What do you mean?" Cheryl asked.

"The medical personnel determined that the wound wasn't made by a bullet," Neal said.

"How did he die, then?"

"We think he was stabbed. We'll have to wait until the autopsy to find out the exact dimensions of the knife, but it was larger than your average switchblade," Carl said.

Oh god. Someone had stabbed Mr. Foster. I felt the color drain from my face. Who on Earth would have wanted to kill a nice old man like him? Had it been a burglar who had broken in and been interrupted by him? That didn't seem right, though. Why break into an apartment on the fifth floor during the middle of the day? Besides, I couldn't remember anything large like the television or the computer missing.

"He had a gun. Couldn't he defend himself?" I said.

"His cataracts would make it difficult to aim," Neal said. "We found two bullet holes in the wall that Mr. Foster was facing. There's no indication that he actually hit his target."

"Why did he have a gun if he couldn't see?" Cheryl said.

"He may have owned the gun before his cataracts got worse," Neal said. "But even if he couldn't see well, it would still be good for intimidation. If his attacker had a knife, he probably thought whoever it was wouldn't try anything if he held them at gunpoint."

Try as I might, I couldn't imagine Mr. Foster firing at anyone, even if he was in danger.

"Why didn't anyone hear the gunshots?" Cheryl asked.

"The gun had a silencer attached. If anyone was home in the adjacent apartments, there's a chance no one would have heard it if the walls were thick enough. If they don't know what a gun sounds like, they wouldn't even know what it was they were hearing," Carl said.

"But…how did they have time to do it?" I said. "It was only ten minutes after I talked to him on the phone that I found him like that."

Carl sighed. "Yes, that's where this gets t[r]
Ten minutes is a very small window of opportuni[ty]
according to the doorman, no one else besides you came in to speak with Mr. Foster."

There was a pause before Cheryl said, "You can't be accusing April. She wouldn't do anything like this. There are plenty of people who can vouch for her. We ran a background check on her and everything when she joined the company."

My throat felt too tight to speak. Me? Kill Mr. Foster? I couldn't imagine kicking a puppy, let alone hurting another human being.

Carl shook his head. "Her story goes along with what Ms. Jones and the doorman told us. We'll check the call logs on her phone for her calls with the victim and the emergency service. Where were you when you received Mr. Foster's call?"

"On a path by the lake shore. It's about five minutes away," I said. "I headed right back after we talked."

"And how long did it take Ms. Jones to hand over the package?"

"She had to inspect my ID and search in the mailroom for it, so...maybe three minutes?" I said.

"And I expect the time it would take to catch the elevator and ride up five floors would add another two minutes," Carl said. I nodded and he continued, "Considering all of this, April would have had less than a minute to murder Mr. Foster. While it is possible to attack someone in such a short time, it would also hint towards premeditation and I don't see enough evidence against Ms. Gladdis to support a motive for that. There should enough here to clear her name. "

I breathed in relief. They didn't suspect me. I couldn't remember a time when I had felt so scared.

"But that leaves us with very little in the way of figuring out new suspects," Neal said. "The culprit could have been another resident of the building who retreated back to their apartment after the murder, but they would have set off the alarm if they had come in through the front door. There's no back door to the apartment, so that eliminates the method of sneaking in by a back way to avoid the lobby. There's also the possibility that someone may have gotten into the apartment before Ms. Gladdis arrived."

"Can't you check the guest registry?" Cheryl said.

"We're in the process of that, but have you ever heard of someone planning to kill a man and signing in first?" Carl said. "Mr. Foster probably didn't know anyone was there until he was confronted."

"So, the murderer was already there when I came in?" I said. The more I thought about it, the more the terrible truth sank in. Someone could have been hiding in the bedroom or the bathroom or one of the closets! Someone could have been waiting for the moment I left and then jumped out and killed Mr. Foster. But why wait for me to leave? I wouldn't be able to put up much of a fight against someone strong enough to overtake Mr. Foster. The murderer could have killed us both. I didn't even want to think about what would have happened to Jesse.

"Not only that, but they could have been there when you came back," Neal said. The detectives and Cheryl were watching me closely, but I was too shocked to say anything. After a moment, he said, "You were very lucky, April."

Carl cleared his throat. "Go home tonight and get some rest. This is a lot to take in." He looked down at Jesse, who had curled up at my feet and fallen asleep, his head lightly resting on my shoelaces. "I think the dog will keep you good company for the time being."

"Thank you for your time, detectives," Cheryl said. She shook their hands and they left us to continue their investigation.

"Are you all right to drive home, April?" Cheryl asked me.

I was as 'all right' as I was ever going to be.

"Yeah," I said. "What's going to happen to Jesse?"

"He'll be taken to a shelter for the night until they can contact a relative to pick him up. Don't worry, he'll be alright," she said. She patted Jesse's head to wake him and took the leash from me. "I'll make sure he gets passed off to the right people. You go home. And don't worry about working tomorrow. We'll treat it like a sick day."

I was grateful for that. After all of this, I wanted

nothing more than to curl up on my couch with the TV on and sleep. I left the wonderfully cool lobby and made my way back to my car. I didn't want to be there when they brought the body out so the ambulance could ship it to wherever. By the time I arrived at my apartment door, it was ten o'clock. Jennifer's door was ajar, just a little. I had the unmistakable urge to knock just so I could see another face and not have to stay alone. What would we talk about? How much of a nightmare my day had become? I had to tell her about it eventually. She wouldn't forgive me for not spilling everything to her. On the other hand, my eyes were barely staying open and I just wanted to collapse. I passed her doorway, which was emitting country ballads from Pandora on her TV, and entered my own quiet apartment.

    The small space was still sweltering. I set my backpack and fanny pack on the coffee table and turned on the windowsill fan as well as the TV for some comforting background noise. My mother sent me a text asking if I was still alive (a daily event if she hasn't heard from me at some point during the day) and I responded that I had made it home in one piece. I'd give it a night before I told my parents the whole story. My stomach growled, but I decided to crash on the couch for a while before I had a late dinner. I blacked out the moment my head hit the cushion.

Chapter 4

At some point in the early morning, my phone lit up and chimed happily. I woke with a start from a dream about bloody carpets and barking dogs and reached for it. It was Jennifer saying that there was a new-edition box-set of the first three seasons of *Grimoire Danya* and asking if I wanted to chip in and buy it.

When I texted her back, I wrote, *We can talk about it later. It's been a crazy night.*

I believe it, she replied. *I'm going to make some brownies after I get home from work this afternoon. You can come over then and tell me about it if you want.*

I told her that it sounded like a great plan and that I would swing by later. My legs were killing me for some reason and I stood to stretch them out. Everything in my apartment looked so alien now, as though I was looking at it through a tinted lens. Maybe my first glimpse at someone freshly dead had screwed with my head. It was different from viewing bodies that had been embalmed and prepared for an open-casket funeral, when they resembled clay dolls rather than the people they once were. James Foster hadn't been dead for more than fifteen minutes when I found him. His skin had still looked pink and warm.

  I couldn't think about that too long or else I would have nothing but nightmares for the next month. I had to do something to keep the thoughts at bay, so I just went to take a shower and go through the rest of my morning routine. When I had parked on the couch with a bowl of cereal in front of some cartoons, my phone rang. It was Cheryl reminding me that I shouldn't even think about working that day.

  "I just want to make sure you have some time to recover," she said.

  "But what about my walks? Do you have enough time to find substitutes?" I said.

  "We'll worry about all of that. You just do what the detectives want you to do and get plenty of rest."

  I wanted to argue and say that I was fine, but I knew she was probably right. I needed time to answer their questions and clear my head. Then I would be refreshed to go back to work the next day.

  "By the way," I began, "Do you know which shelter Jesse was taken to?"

  "The Evanston Humane Society," Cheryl said. "I

helped drop him off. They'll contact James Foster's family and arrange for someone to take him."

"Do you know if he had any family in Chicago? He never mentioned them," I said.

"He had a couple of emergency contacts in his profile, I think. One was a neighbor and the other was his landlord. He didn't list any family," Cheryl said.

So we didn't have any idea who Jesse would be living with now. "Do you think they would let me visit him?"

"I don't see why not," Cheryl said. "You were his walker, after all. Give him an extra pat for me while you're there!"

That made me feel a little better. It would give me something to do with the morning. I finished breakfast and threw on some clothes before heading out. I was so used to dressing in sweats that any time I went outside in jeans and brand-clothing, I felt overdressed. For today, I just slipped on a pair of blue denim pants and a white, V-necked shirt. I went to my car and did a search on my GPS for the Evanston Humane Society. Luckily, the building had a bright, blue sign with a paw print next to its logo, so it wasn't difficult to find.

The lobby was lined with bulletin boards holding pictures and profiles of adoptable pets. In the corners, there were shelves of flea and tick medications for sale. A few people sat in a waiting area with pets that were either being checked in or out of the vet's office that operated in the same building. I went up to the woman behind the front desk and asked if any Pointers named Jesse had been admitted since the day before.

"Ah yes, we did receive a dog matching that description after his owner passed away," she said. "Are you a relative of the family?"

Passed away. They made it sound tame.

"No, I'm not related to his owner, but he was my client for about three months. I was his dog walker," I said. "I was wondering if I could visit Jesse while he's in here?"

The receptionist smiled. "Of course. He would probably love a familiar face."

An assistant led me into a wide hallway with crates and cages built into the walls. Each one had food and water bowls as well as padded beds. Most of the inhabitants began barking or meowing at me as I passed. Some crowded against the front of their cages and watched me with huge, pleading eyes. It broke my heart to be in adoption centers like this. My first inclination was to take all of them home with me and love them forever.

Jesse was pacing in an alcove with a grated door. He kept pausing and shaking out his fur. I knew that body language; he was feeling overwhelmed and nervous. I went up to the door and called his name. He trotted over to me, wagging his tail in excitement. The assistant opened the door and my arms were suddenly filled with ninety-five pounds of dog. He put his front paws on my arms and licked every inch of my face his tongue could reach.

"I missed you too, boy! Are they taking good care of you?" I asked him. He responded by whimpering.

"He's been an angel so far, except when he's in there alone. He gets so nervous," the assistant said.

"He's used to being around people," I said. "I think his father worked from home, so they were usually together."

I set Jesse's front paws on the ground and dug out a couple of spare treats I found in my pocket. He gobbled them up gladly. He was still wearing the collar with the silver cylinder Mr. Foster had bought for him. I hadn't noticed it before, but the cylinder had a seam running around one end like a thermos. I twisted it open to look inside, but it was empty. Maybe the tracker was a separate piece. But where was it now?

"Have you seen a container like this before?" I asked the assistant.

"Not while I've worked here, but my neighbor's dog had one like it," she said.

"I think they're for tracking devices? That's what Jesse's owner told me, but I don't know for sure," I said.

"That would make sense," she said. "Some people may be nervous about having their dogs microchipped."

That was interesting. Maybe Mr. Foster was squeamish about having one placed in Jesse. But if that was the case, then why was the cylinder empty?

"Does he have anyone coming to pick him up?" I

asked.

"A couple members of the family are scheduled to come in tomorrow and claim him." She scratched behind Jesse's ears as she spoke. His tail was wagging non-stop from all the attention.

After a few more minutes of showering Jesse with love, I sighed and stood up to go. The assistant guided him back into his cubby. He whimpered and stared up at me with woeful eyes. I silently promised I would come back and then headed to the lobby.

I had no idea what to do with myself for the rest of the day, to be honest. Dog walking had become the basis around which every other aspect of my life was structured. My daily routine went like this: wake up, do morning yoga, eat breakfast, walk dogs, have lunch, walk more dogs, come home, eat dinner, sleep. Sometimes I hung out with Jennifer in the evening if we had time and she didn't want me to be stuck eating a microwavable supper from a box. She would be at theater practice for most of today and I didn't really have any other friends in the city that I could just casually hang out with. I would be lying if I said that this was how I had expected my life to turn out.

Not that I was complaining too much. Walking dogs got me out of the house and breathing fresh air. Not to mention the fact that it was very hard to feel under-appreciated when the doggies or kitties I visited greeted me enthusiastically at the door. It was just starting to bother me that I had so little time or opportunity to meet some human friends.

When I got back to my apartment, I realized that this would be the perfect opportunity to call my family and tell them the entire story. Part of me wondered why I had waited so long, but there was a worry in the back of my mind that my parents would freak out over the news that I had found a dead body and try to convince me to return home. My mother was nervous about me living in the city as it was.

As it turned out, I was putting all of my worries in the wrong places. When I called my mother, she was more worried about me being paranoid and afraid. I didn't feel too bad, though I have to admit that while I spoke to her, I was more relaxed than I had been in days, like I was suddenly standing on more solid ground. I guess there's something soothing about listening to a parent's voice while you were stressed. Toby, my little brother, thought that the entire thing sounded too weird to be true. I told him I agreed, even when I had been the one in the middle of it all. When he asked if I was going to be in any newspapers, I mentioned that kind of publicity was probably the last thing Best Furry Friends needed.

They offered to come and visit me in case I was feeling nervous, but I told them there was no rush to do it immediately. I wasn't so unsettled that I felt the need to tear them away from their work just to spend a couple of days with me in the middle of the week. Maybe in a week or two, if I started feeling out of sorts again.

As she promised she would, Jennifer texted me and said she had gotten home from work in the afternoon and asked if I wanted to come over. I was getting restless and searching for another distraction, so I said I would be right over. Jennifer's apartment smelled like vanilla scented candles and baking chocolate. The heavenly scent hit me the moment I opened the door and made me realize I hadn't eaten much all day except for the cereal that morning.

"Hey there! You're just in time. The brownies are almost done!" Jennifer said as she rounded the corner of the hallway that led to the living room. She trailed off when she saw me. "Wow, did you have to walk fifty dogs today or what? You look exhausted!"

"Something like that," I said, taking a seat on the same leather couch that had hidden the silverfish the day before. That felt like a million years ago.

"Lemme get the goods and you can tell me all about it," she said. She disappeared back into the kitchen and brought out a silver plate packed with big chunks of chocolate fudge brownies that tasted incredible and warmed me inside. Jennifer, as I had predicted, wanted to hear every detail of whatever it was that had happened. Luckily for her, I wasn't under the same shock as when I had told my story to the detectives and I could remember most of the details. When I got to the part where I had found Mr. Foster's body, Jennifer's face transformed into a look of horror and she stared at me.

"Oh my god, did you call the police?"

I nodded. "Of course. That's why I got back so late," I said.

"I had no idea," Jennifer said, covering her mouth

with one slim hand. "That's horrible! Are you sure you're okay?"

It was sweet that everyone was so worried about me, but I wasn't used to the attention and it was making me self-conscious. I assured her that I was fine and then glossed over the rest of the events up until getting back home.

"I should bring you some lunch or something tomorrow. Some comfort food is never a bad thing," she said.

Despite everything that had happened, I laughed. "You're too nice. You don't have to do that for me."

"I just know that if all that had happened to me, I would be too freaked out to move," she said. "Didn't the detectives say the murderer was still there? What if something awful had happened to you?!"

I looked down, feeling the heat drain from my face. I didn't want to be reminded of that particular point. As though she could sense that she had made a mistake, she said, quickly, "I'm sorry! I didn't mean to scare you, it's just..."

"It's all right. I'll probably just be heading to bed soon anyway. I'm going back to my route tomorrow," I said, before getting up.

"So what happened to the dog?" Jennifer asked.

"He was taken to the Humane Society in Evanston," I said. "I went up to visit him this morning."

"That poor thing. He must be so confused. Do you think pets even realize when their owners die?" she said.

I shrugged, but really, I had started to wonder the same thing. Mr. Foster had loved Jesse and Jesse had always stayed by his master's side. Even if he didn't understand the concept of death, it probably wouldn't take him long to realize something was wrong. That made my heart hurt for him even more.

"Well, it's a good thing you're around to make him feel better. And I'm glad you had some time off! I hope it helped get your mind off of...you know..." Jennifer trailed off, but I knew what she was getting at.

"Yeah, it did. Thanks," I said and hugged her. "It's going to be weird going back to work."

"Do you think the other walkers will want to ask questions?" Jennifer said. "Do you even get to talk to them much?"

I shook my head. "Not really. Sometimes we text each other if we have a crazy story, but that's about it."

"Well, this story is plenty crazy. Just don't let them get to you if you don't want to talk about it anymore."

"I won't," I assured her. She put half the brownies into a tupperware container for me to take. It was dark out when I finally said goodbye and went back to my apartment. I stuffed the container in the fridge and got ready for bed. When I finally tucked myself in, the same questions Jennifer had asked swirled through my mind. Do animals know when their owners die? Jesse had always been so happy-go-lucky. I couldn't imagine him being sad. His life with his loving master couldn't have been more perfect.

That night, I had my first nightmare since the murder. I was in Foster's room again with Jesse cowering beside me. Except he wasn't looking at Mr. Foster's bloody body on the carpet, but at something lurking behind us. I heard the sound of metal against metal, like a sword from *Grimoire Danya* being unsheathed. I turned around slowly and screamed when something silver and sharp sped towards me.

I was back in my bed, gasping for air a moment later, with my sheets bunched at my feet. A quick glance at the clock told me it was three in the morning. I groaned and rubbed my eyes, wishing I had taken a sleeping pill earlier. It was going to be a long night.

Chapter 5

My first walks of the day were with a Maltese and a Great Dane puppy. The Maltese was tiny, only a little bit bigger than my hand, and had white fur that felt more like down. I didn't stay out too long with her since the sun was quickly heating up the concrete and I didn't want her little paws to burn. Whenever I picked her up to carry her up and down the stairs that she couldn't manage on her own, she would pant on me with breath that smelled suspiciously like Fritos.

The Great Dane puppy was growing up fast. Every day I came back, he would be just a little bit bigger and his legs just a little bit more long and gangly. At first, it had taken him a while to get used to his new body. He would stumble over himself in his haste to get outside and would amble along the sidewalk beside me. He was already taller than most dogs would be in their entire lifetimes.

Next came two roly-poly pugs with flab just about everywhere on their bodies. They snorted up a storm while I put on their harnesses and leashes. It didn't take them long to get tired on their walk and soon they were breathing hard enough that I decided it would be safest to take them back home. When I sat on the couch to drink a glass of water, they immediately hopped up next to me and settled on my lap. On a day with a lighter schedule, I would have rather had my teeth pulled than have to nudge them off so I could leave.

The pugs would never have been able to make it up the steps of the apartment building where the next client lived. The landlord of the complex kept the lobby pristine, with waxed hardwood floors and walls decorated with landscape paintings and potted spider plants. He lived under the constant fear that the dogs in the building would go barreling up and down the steps and upturn everything. For that reason, pets were only allowed to go through the back doors of the apartments.

Of course, the client I was visiting just had to live on the top floor of the building, which meant I was forced to climb four grueling flights of stairs outside in the heat and humidity. I took my time making my way up, trying to repress any bitter thoughts that bubbled up to the surface. Did they honestly think that their thick-coated huskies enjoyed doing this whenever they had a walk?

When I reached the top, I glanced over the wooden railing of the balcony at the dark asphalt below. The wooden platforms did a good job of obscuring the balconies above and below. They would have to, or else anyone would be tempted to steal the grills and lawn chairs that some people left outside. It must have been great for privacy if anyone just wanted to sit outside and read a book or visit with someone.

It wasn't until halfway through the walk with the dogs when it occurred to me that outdoor structures like back staircases would be the perfect place for someone to get into a building undetected. Mr. Foster's apartment building was sleek and glossy, not a place for wooden scaffolding. However, every apartment building was required to have a fire escape by law. Wouldn't that be the perfect place for a killer to hide and not have to deal with the doorman? I couldn't remember seeing a back door to a fire escape while I was visiting Jesse, but maybe the stairs led to one of the windows instead.

Unfortunately, there was no way to investigate it now. I couldn't very well go tromping back to the building and ask if I could have another look around the place. I wondered if that kind of thing had ever occurred to the detectives. They were probably one step ahead of me, but if I met them again, I supposed I could ask.

I distracted myself from thinking about poor Mr. Foster and that horrible incident by imagining how Jesse would act when he saw me later on that day. I had planned on visiting him the moment I got off work. I couldn't stand the thought of leaving him alone without all the treats and petting he wanted!

It wasn't until my afternoon walk with Stella, the very stubborn terrier, that I realized that my thoughts had never been very far from Jesse all day long. I was always wondering how he was doing, whether he was bored, or what they were feeding him. I was hard put not to run over to the Humane Society in the middle of my lunch hour but I steadfastly waited until my last walk was done before heading up north.

The receptionist was the same one from the day before and she let me into the back with no worries. Jesse was curled up on the padded bed in his cubby when I came in, staring through the bars of his cubby at a muscular Rottweiler on the other side of the hall that was whining at him. When I came into view, he stood up and started wriggling around with excitement. He almost bowled me over when the assistant finally let him out.

"Has he had any other visitors?" I asked, when I could open my mouth without fear of him sticking his tongue down my throat.

"Besides you? Not yet, I'm afraid," the assistant said. "Though today is supposed to be the day when the family comes by to claim him."

It's about time, I thought. He doesn't deserve to be left in here. Jesse had flopped to the ground and rolled onto his back, exposing his spotted belly for me to rub. After a long moment, the door at the end of the hall opened and a small group of people came in.

The assistant with me said, "I'm sorry, but we're only allowed to let one of the dogs out at a time. Jesse will have to go back in if they're going to be looking at the animals."

"It's okay. He's the one we're here to see." I

recognized the voice instantly since I had been obsessed with its owner for almost a year. When I stood up and turned, it felt like I was emerging from a lake of ice. I have to say, seeing Rick Weaver in normal clothes was...weird, especially up close. A smattering of fresh stubble was growing on his chin, which meant he was going to be filming for another episode of *Grimoire Danya* soon. He looked paler than I had ever seen him on camera and the dark circles under his eyes weren't make-up. Something must have been stressing him to make him look so worn out.

Beside him was Mark Bishop with his hair in the short, dark style he had worn through most of the recent season. He was growing out his stubble like Rick was and was actually wearing a shirt that covered his bronzed chest, for once. He looked just as tired as Rick, with a subtle tightness around his mouth and eyes.

I took a deep breath and said, "Uh, hi."

"Hey there," Rick said. He smiled and for a second, his face almost returned to its normal color. "So, I assume you know Jesse?"

"I...worked for Mr. Foster. I walked him...um, Jesse, I mean," I said rapidly.

"Oh, I see," Rick said. "Grandpa hasn't been feeling too good recently. I'm glad you were able to help him out."

I just nodded in a stupor. His face was far too beautiful for me to look anywhere else. There may as well have been a frame of roses straight out of a cartoon around him. Jesse scurried over to Mark, who crouched down beside him and petted him.

"It's been a while, hasn't it, boy?" he said. "I haven't seen him in years. When was the last time they came to a family reunion?"

"Five years, I think. Jesse was still a puppy," Rick said, watching them.

At some point during this exchange, my brain finally kicked in and processed what they were saying.

"Did you say grandpa? Mr. Foster was your grandfather?" I said.

"Yeah, but we didn't get to see him too often," Rick said, his smile fading.

I hadn't even realized that Rick and Mark were related, let alone that they were part of James Foster's family. Mark's hair and skin tone were markedly darker than Rick's. Rick was taller, but Mark had a leaner build and his features were more aquiline. I couldn't see as much of a resemblance there. Maybe they were half-brothers or Mark was adopted. They had always been tight-lipped about their personal lives.

Now that I had the chance to think about it, I could see some similarities between them and Mr. Foster. In Rick's face was James Foster's strong jawline and slightly arched eyebrows. The hints were all there, I just never made the connection.

I wanted to ask some more questions, it might be awkward if I started grilling them about their family before I had even told them my name.

"Well, I'm very sorry for your loss. Um...I'm April Gladdis," I said, holding my hand out to Rick. "I love *Grimoire Danya*. I have the DVD's and everything."

Rick took my hand in a firm grip. "Oh! You watch the series. Thanks. I love meeting fans."

"I've always wanted to meet you," I blurted out. "I've been watching it for, like, two years. I've even seen the secret episode where Dyllas killed the Ice Dragon."

"Oh yeah, I remember that one. It wasn't actually supposed to be released outside of the DVD's, but it got leaked early," Rick said. When he had pulled his hand away from mine, I could have sworn the temperature dropped a few degrees.

Mark stood up and Jesse stared at Rick expectantly. After a moment of vain waiting, he came back beside me and plopped down.

"We're actually hoping to get the next season started up soon, but we've kinda...run into some trouble," Mark said.

"Really? What's wrong?" I said, before I realized they might not actually want to tell me any of that stuff. They probably wouldn't be thrilled to have a nosey fan poking around their business.

"Oh, just money issues. Nothing to worry about," Rick said. "And this thing with our grandfather."

Thing with their grandfather. Neither of them

sounded too broken up about his death. Maybe they weren't as attached to him as I had been with my grandparents. Mr. Foster had never mentioned them and I would have thought that having celebrity grandsons would be something to brag about.

"I hate to rush this, but we should probably get to deciding what to do with the dog," Rick said.

I wanted to stay and talk with them some more, but this sounded like a private thing. I said goodbye and went to the lobby. Would it be overly creepy if I waited to ask if they had more time to chat? I settled in a chair in the corner of the room and grabbed the nearest copy of *Animal Wellness*. I stared at an advertisement for flea medication for a full fifteen minutes before they came back out, notably without Jesse. While they spoke to the receptionist, I held the magazine higher to hide my face.

Before I knew it, they were both heading towards the front door. I buried myself further into the chair until the swishing of the glass doors announced that they had left. I didn't understand. Why wasn't Jesse with them? Were they going to pick him up later?

I casually set the magazine down and followed them outside. Unfortunately, they were headed for the opposite end of the parking lot from where my car was. Maybe if I pretended that my car was parked on their side, I could catch up to them. I hurried down the sidewalk until I was almost to where they were. They had stopped in between two polished, black cars to talk with each other. Rick was leaning against the side of a Porsche so casually that I knew it must have been his. I had no idea that they were able to support themselves so...luxuriously from the income they made from the web series.

I strode towards them and waved. "Hello again!"

Both of them looked up at the same time. They wore such serious expressions that I almost turned on my heel and ran away.

Mark smiled thinly. "Oh, hey. I didn't think you would stick around."

"I was just curious," I said. "I still wanted to ask you about Mr. Foster."

Rick's expression darkened even further. This was definitely not the kind of reaction I was hoping for.

"What do you want to ask?" he said.

"Well, it's just that he never mentioned the series before..." I said.

"I'm not really surprised," Rick said. "He didn't take a whole lot of interest in our projects."

"Oh," I said, mentally flailing for a moment. "So are you going to take Jesse home with you?"

Mark shrugged. "I'm afraid no one in our family is interested in keeping him. We were the only ones who bothered to come and see him here."

"Are you kidding?" I asked. "But, he's so nice!"

"I'm sure he is," Rick said. "But grandpa had some bad feelings towards our mother and she didn't want to take the dog when it would bring back nasty memories."

"I don't understand. Mr. Foster was always friendly when I talked to him," I said.

Rick smiled wryly. "Well, that's nice. At least he was good to someone, for once."

"What do you mean?" I said.

Mark waved the question aside. "It's a long story. You don't have to worry about it."

I was dying to know more, but I let it go. "Are you sure you don't want to keep Jesse?"

"I can't. My apartment building won't allow pets," Mark said.

When I looked at Rick, he shrugged. "I'm allergic. I wouldn't be able to keep him if I wanted to."

These guys were breaking my heart. For the longest time, I had imagined Rick and me getting together at a convention and moving to a small house somewhere in suburban Illinois. We would keep all the cats and dogs we wanted. In the summertime, we would let the dogs run around in our fenced back yard and then in the winter, we would curl up with the cats by the fireplace. Now that fantasy was shattering. Well, every relationship had its compromises, so I heard. We might still be able to make it work, right?

"So what's going to happen to him?" I asked.

"We told them to put Jesse up for adoption. If we can't take care of him, someone else can," Rick said.

"Yeah, just because our family had issues with his

dad doesn't mean he can't be happy," Mark said.

"So...anyone can take him?" I asked.

"I think so. Why? Are you interested?" Rick said.

"Yeah, actually. I would love to take him," I said, not skipping a beat. Never mind that my apartment was way too small to be keeping a dog his size and that I was barely supporting myself paycheck to paycheck. I could make it work. I didn't want to think about the kind of family that Jesse could end up with. He should be with someone better than that, no matter what his father had apparently done to piss off the rest of the family.

"I'm sure you can go back in and talk to the receptionist," Mark said. "They might be able to set you up."

I thanked them and watched as they pulled out their keys and started unlocking their cars. Crap, I hadn't even been able to talk about *Grimoire Danya* as much as I had wanted to! They might not want to talk about their personal lives, but I still wanted to hear about the series.

"Hey, um, it was really nice meeting you. I really meant it when I said I love your work," I said, hoping I didn't sound desperate.

Rick turned and gave me the warmest smile I had seen out of him yet. "Thanks. We've got some good stuff planned for it."

"Are you guys going to any conventions soon?" I asked.

They both paused, thinking. "We'll be at a couple in September and October, I think. One's in Chicago and the other is in Tennessee."

If I saved up and planned for it, I might just be able to make it to the one in Chicago. Tennessee was right out. I didn't have the kind of time and money it would take to make it all the way out there. My chances of seeing them again in person were looking bleak.

Rick seemed to catch onto my disappointment. "Tell you what, though," he began, "I wanted to thank you for looking after Jesse. He meant a lot to the old man. We're going to be filming part of the next episode of *Grimoire Danya* this Saturday at noon. If you want, you can come to the studio and sit in during the shoot."

"Seriously?" I said, breathlessly. This was too good to be true! "I won't be in the way or anything?"

"I don't see a problem with it," he said. "I can't promise it will be all that entertaining, but if you're interested, then sure."

"Um, if it's alright with you, I have a friend who loves the series too. Could I bring her along?" I asked, hoping I wasn't overstepping my bounds. Jennifer would love watching them film as much as I would.

Mark and Rick glanced at each other. "Sure, just as long as there isn't a big crowd," Rick said.

"No! No, of course not!" I said, quickly. "It'll be just the two of us, I swear. We won't bother anybody."

Mark gave me a small smile. "If you're going to be

there on Saturday, I can bring you some of the dog's stuff from grandpa's place. The place is being cleaned out now."

"Really? That would help a lot! Thank you," I said, relieved. While I wasn't too worried about being able to support a dog as big as Jesse, I wasn't about to turn away free supplies for him, especially when they were the toys and beds that Jesse would be used to already.

I watched as they climbed into their cars and drove out of the parking lot. I had survived that a lot better than I thought I would! Certainly, I had stammered less than I had been expecting.

I went back into the Humane Society and made my request to adopt Jesse. They were already in the process of putting his name through the system. It took a bit of paperwork and an interview, but an hour later, I had a very big dog in the passenger's seat of my car. I needed to get dog supplies for the next few days, so I found the nearest pet shop on my GPS and headed out. Jesse braced himself against the front of the seat when we started moving. I turned off the AC and rolled down the windows half way so he could relax with some fresh air. He immediately stuck his head out to sniff the wind and observe other dogs barking at him from their own cars.

When I wasn't idling behind an obnoxiously long stoplight and petting Jesse to put him at ease, I was thinking back on the boys. Call me crazy, but I hadn't expected them to be the kind of people to lack compassion for the recently deceased. Maybe this meeting had just been a snag and stress was causing them to act more reserved. I remembered seeing them so optimistic and courteous to the reporters during interviews. How much of that had been an act just like the work they did on set? The cameras would pick up the image they wanted their audience to believe.

      I didn't understand why Mr. Foster would be so reclusive, either. What would make him distance himself from his own flesh and blood? Maybe he was just a wealthy old man wanting to spend the rest of his days alone. But if he was just minding his own business, who would have been furious enough to want him dead?

      I took Jesse into the pet shop with me, silently blessing their open-door policy for animals. I would have felt terrible leaving him in the car. He sniffed everything in sight and stopped near the bird cages to watch them flutter around.

      I loaded up a shopping cart with dog food, bowls and a large, padded dog bed. Everything was the cheapest I could find and only temporary. I just wanted it to last until I could get the rest of his supplies out of Foster's apartment. After everything was paid for, I loaded up the car and drove back home.

      I meandered around the front gate with Jesse, giving him a potty break and a chance to get used to all of the new scents. I glanced at my landlord's office with a sense of dread. Eventually, I was going to have to inform him of my apartment's newest occupant and hope he didn't raise my rent too much.

      The evening was spent trying to help Jesse settle

in. I had been worried that my apartment was too claustrophobic for a dog his size, but Jesse didn't seem uncomfortable. He didn't have nearly as much roaming room as before, but we could make up for that by going to the park.

I sent Cheryl a message about Jesse, figuring she would be interested in the new arrangement. The company wouldn't stop caring about the dog, even if his owner wasn't around anymore.

Cheryl answered my message and called me after dinner to see how things were going.

"He's doing pretty well. He doesn't have much of an appetite, though," I said. He had barely touched the food in his bowl. "But he's been curious about everything else. He's so friendly...I don't know why the family didn't want him."

"Well, I'm sure he will be in good hands from now on," Cheryl said. "If you go anywhere and need someone to watch him, you know who to call."

I laughed at that. "Do I get a discount?"

"I'm sure we can knock down the price since you've worked so hard," she said. "By the way, a couple of the other walkers in your area are over-scheduled tomorrow. I was wondering if you could take an appointment with Spot Maxwell."

Spot was a chubby Jack Russell terrier who I had only walked once before. He was located a bit further south than my route usually took me, but not so far that it would be inconvenient.

"I should be able to fit him in," I replied.

"Great, thanks a lot. Just call up tomorrow and we can make sure you get his key," she said.

We said good night and hung up. I wanted to tell Jennifer everything that had happened at the Humane Society as soon as I could, but she had work that evening. I debated on whether to tell her in person or message her now. It might lighten up her day if work at the cafe was slow. I opted to send her a text.

You'll never guess who got invited to a live film shoot for Grimoire Danya on Saturday.

It wasn't until Jesse and I went for our evening walk that I received her reply.

OMG HOW DID YOU DO THAT???

I laughed and typed out, *Turns out Rick and Mark are James Foster's grandsons.*

That's insane. I had no idea, she said.

Neither did I until I met them and they told me, I said.

YOU MET THEM? WHERE?

I was visiting Jesse in the humane society. They came to put him up for adoption because no one in the family wanted him, so I took him.

Omg that's crazy! so jealous. they must be so cute! so you have the dog now? I will be home at 5 tomorrow.

You have to tell me everything!!

Will do, I replied. When she didn't send another message, I assumed she had returned to work.

Jesse was perched on the sofa, gazing out of the smudged windows behind it. If I actually cared about pets jumping all over my furniture, I would have chased him off. Every once in a while, he would make a high-pitched whimper and peer over at me with anxious eyes.

I went over and sat next to him, scratching his back. It had been two whole days since he had been separated from his master. Some dogs would panic if their owners were gone for five minutes. As far as I knew, James had never been away from home for very long. This time, he wasn't coming back at all. I couldn't imagine what must be going through Jesse's mind.

When it was time for bed, I put down his big pillow and covered it with a blanket for extra padding. Jesse sniffed at the cushion and then hesitantly laid down. It wasn't until I had crawled into my own bed when I heard a rustle and felt the mattress tip as it accommodated Jesse's weight. James must have let him sleep on his bed, too. In a few minutes, he was already snoring away.

Chapter 6

    The next day, I checked and double-checked that he had everything he could possibly need before I left. His food and water bowls were full, his toys were out in the open, and the TV was on at a low volume so he wouldn't feel so alone. I was worried that he would start yelping or whining the way some dogs did the second their owners stepped out of the door. If Jesse had that sort of separation anxiety and disturbed the neighbors, my landlord would give me an earful.

    I finished up my usual morning route of puppies and huskies before I headed home for lunch and found out just what kind of anxiety Jesse suffered from. After he bombarded me with wet, slobbery kisses at the door, I gently pushed him away to discover the shredded remains of a pair of tennis shoes in the entryway. The living room was covered with the white, fluffy innards of a pillow my mom had given me when I first moved into the apartment.

Hopefully, he hadn't been too loud during his path of destruction.

I sat down among the remains of the gutted pillow and sighed. He would have to be kept in a crate until I could trust that he wouldn't tear the place to shreds while I was gone. I used to think that people who crated their dogs were cruel until I learned that crates were for dogs what man-caves were for men. It gave them their own personal territories and it was good for the owners' furniture.

Once most of the mess had been cleaned, I put Jesse's harness on and took him around the block. A routine was starting to emerge already. He insisted on marking every other tree until I started worrying about the time and dragged him back home.

I set his food and water bowls in the bathroom and pulled down all the towels so he wouldn't be tempted to use them as a chew toy. He could stay in there until I came back that evening. I lured him in with a treat and shut the door behind me. It only took a moment for him to start whimpering and scrabbling at the door. My heart would crack in half if I listened to it much longer, so I grabbed my stuff and flew out the door.

I went to do my afternoon visits in the suffocating humidity. By the end of each outing, the dogs would be lolling their tongues and they would be panting hard enough to make small whirlwinds. I hoped the tiles on my bathroom floor stay cool enough to keep Jesse comfortable. I was suddenly grateful that I had the habit of leaving the bathroom window open during the summer to let in a breeze. It was high off the ground since I lived on the third floor, so I wasn't worried about anyone breaking in.

It was late afternoon when I finally met with Spot's regular walker to get his key. Spot lived in a two-story originally intended to be a duplex. The owners had bought the entire thing out and transformed it into their home. Spot wasn't allowed on the second floor where the antiques and special furniture were kept, but he had the first floor to himself.

He met me at the door when he heard the key jingling in the lock, but he hesitated when he saw that it was a new walker. I crouched down and offered him a treat, speaking in the googly, baby talk that meant I was friendly. He hesitated and took the treat before his nose was suddenly glued to my shoes and my fanny pack. I grabbed his leash and hooked it onto his collar. They didn't use a harness, but to be honest, I doubted he could get too far even if he was able to escape from the leash. Every time he shook out his fur, his belly fat rolls jiggled. We would take it easy in the heat and come back early to play in the AC. I didn't want him to have a doggie heart attack.

To my amazement, Spot became more animated outside, with a spring in his step as he trotted along beside me. He was one of those tiny dogs who thought they could take on a bear if they wanted to. He was constantly on the lookout for rabbits and squirrels. If he saw some leaves twitching, he would freeze and perk up his ears until I tugged at the leash to refocus his attention on the walk.

We were passing by a house surrounded by a dense ring of bushes when Spot suddenly decided that he was going to be a hunting dog. He must have heard a rustle underneath a large, jagged pine bush behind us, because without warning, his narrow head slipped free of his collar and he darted away. By the time I looked back, he had already torn across the lawn until his front half was buried in the bushes.

I called out his name and lunged for his hind legs before they vanished within the underbrush. He backed out and peered up at me with a toothy grin. I slid the collar back over his neck and tightened it until I could be sure he wouldn't escape again. All the while, the little rascal was constantly scanning the bushes, looking for any sign of his quarry. With some treat-bribery, I was eventually able to negotiate him back to the sidewalk.

A handful of brown, spiny burrs stuck to his face and neck, but he didn't act as though it was painful. While he gobbled up his biscuits, I started picking them out of his fur. I was digging out a stubborn burr from underneath his collar when I noticed a silver cylinder hanging from his license ring. It was the same size and shape as the one attached to Jesse's collar. I tried to remember if any of the dogs on my regular route had one, but no one came to mind. I would have to pay better attention during the next few days.

Now curious, I opened it up like I had with Jesse's, expecting to see some kind of tracking chip that maybe the other one had been missing. It was completely empty, except for a few white ridges. I ran my pinky just inside the rim and it came away with a fine powder. Other than biscuit residue or dust from the factory that had produced the cylinder, I had no idea what it could be.

    I wiped my hand on my shorts and closed the cylinder. Spot was standing there patiently, panting as though he had run a 5k. I took him home and put a handful of ice in his water bowl. He curled up in a dog bed in the corner of the living room and promptly fell asleep.

    I wrote a note for his parents (discreetly omitting the part where his collar came off) and headed out. Before I got back to my apartment, I went to the pet shop from the day before to pick up a crate. I only had a vague idea what I was looking for without knowing Jesse's exact measurements. I was able to guess what size would be right by eyeballing the crates they had set up on display. It was a black, wire-framed box that would give him plenty of room to stand up and turn around without being restrictive. I would pull the dog bed and tuck his water bowl in the corner to make it more comfortable.

    My stomach had started niggling me for dinner. I was getting so much exercise with this job that I was constantly hungry. I should consider keeping a cooler in my car for extra food. With plans for dinner bouncing around my head, I went back to my apartment. All was quiet on the inside, which made me worried. Jesse was laying on his side in the bathroom when I checked on him. He lifted up his head and peered at me, his tail thumping against the tile as it wagged. He had made a huge dent in the layer of food in his bowl. That was a good sign that his appetite was returning, at least.

He wandered out to the living room and jumped onto the couch, easily taking up half of it if he was stretched out. I knew I should take him for a walk, but my legs were feeling rubbery from all the walks I'd already had that day. Besides, I didn't have the heart to drag Jesse off the couch just yet. I sat down beside him and used a remote to flick on the TV. I petted his neck and he laid his head on my leg. Suddenly, he slid off the couch and slunk off into the bare corner beside the entertainment center with his tail tucked between his legs. He sat down, facing the wall.

"Jesse?" I said, mystified. I clapped my hands, trying to coax him back. "What's the matter? Come here."

He didn't budge. Was he trying to get back at me for locking him up in the bathroom? He had been fine a moment ago. I tried scratching his ears and offering him a bacon treat, but he ignored me. Maybe he was feeling defensive because he smelled the scent of a new dog, but considering how many other dogs he must have smelled on me before he came to live here, that didn't make sense.

"Look, I'm sorry for putting you in the bathroom, but I can't just let you tear the place up," I said, reaching up to stroke his nose. He turned his head away and growled.

"Okay, fine, be a grouch," I said. There wasn't much more I could do at this point aside from giving him some space until he got over this funk.

I made a quick dinner and then took a shower to

soothe my sore muscles. When I came out, I was dressed in yoga shorts and a loose t-shirt. Jesse was napping on the couch.

"Are you ready for a walk or are you still mad?" I asked, jingling his leash. He immediately scrambled off the couch and sat down next to me.

"Sure, now you're friendly," I said. He didn't snuffle or look away while I came close to hook on his leash. He didn't even growl when I adjusted his collar. Even more puzzling was the way he cuddled up next to me after the walk when we were lazing around and watching my nightly game shows. He was acting very strange tonight. Maybe he was having mood swings because he missed his father.

When I went to bed, I patted the space beside my feet and he jumped up. If I had thought he was a couch-hog, he was worse on the bed. He sprawled out his legs and left me with a thin strip of space close to the edge. I nudged him over so that I could work the covers loose. At least having Jesse close by kept the nightmares away for a night.

In the morning, Jesse watched as I moved the couch over and set up the crate where he would be able to see the rest of the room. I tucked his water bowl in the corner, slightly underneath a corner of the dog bed so it would be held in place. Jesse made no move towards the door, even when I gave him an encouraging nudge. He sniffed at the huge pillow and looked back at me, confused. This was going to be harder than I thought. He had probably been free-running in Foster's apartment since he was a puppy. I rubbed his back soothingly and kept talking to him softly to urge him inside.

It took placing a kong toy (a hollow, bulbous, rubber tube) with peanut butter towards the back of the crate before Jesse was willing to go in. I shut and secured the door behind him. He took it in turns to lick the peanut butter and stare at me as I got ready to go back to work. I switched the TV on and slipped out the front door quietly. I paused and listened at the door. Jesse was so busy with the kong, he hadn't started whimpering. I was grateful he didn't bark or whine like some of the other dogs I visited that suffered from major separation anxiety. That always made me feel horrible.

Case in point, the Great Dane puppy, named Admiral, seemed to be developing a streak of anxiety lately. One of his owners had left for a long business trip that weekend and apparently the one that left was the one he had attached himself to the most. His other parent was at work and he was feeling lonely in his big house. I could hear him whining and scrabbling at the door to his crate before I reached the first porch step. At least Jesse wasn't the only one confined on such a beautiful day.

Admiral was already starting to figure out our routine. He had his favorite spot outside to go to for his bathroom break and he knew that it was lunchtime when we returned. If I wasn't moving towards the food bin quick enough, he would start nudging his bowl in my direction. Today, he actually chewed lightly on the rim as though he was going to pick it up and show it to me. I giggled and obediently gave him a cup of food.

When it was time for Admiral to go back into his crate, I put a couple of small, meaty treats inside and he pounced in. It was never a good idea to force a dog into a crate because they would start associating the crate with anxiety. It was a fortunate thing neither Admiral nor Jesse were giving me a hard time. *Unfortunately*, it didn't stop the poor puppy from whimpering as soon as I was out of sight. I hoped he wasn't going to be by himself for much longer.

While I finished my route, I kept a look out for more those silver cylinders like the ones I saw Jesse and Spot wearing on their collars. None of my other dogs had them, oddly enough. It was rare that I saw the other dog walkers, so I wouldn't have the chance to ask them, either. When I had some down time in the afternoon, I sent a message to Cheryl, wondering if she might know anything about the weird trinkets. She said she didn't know what I was talking about. I was hitting dead ends all over the place. There hadn't even been a manufacturer's mark anywhere on Jesse's cylinder, so I couldn't look it up on the internet. There was nothing more I could do but keep my eyes peeled.

That evening, Jennifer peered out of her door when she heard me get back to my apartment. I wasn't surprised. The walls seemed paper-thin sometimes.

"How were your rehearsals?"

"Good," she said, grinning. "But that sounds boring compared to your day! You have to tell me all about the boys! Where did you meet them? What did they say?"

I chuckled. "I'll tell you everything but I should check on Jesse real quick."

"So, the dog is in your apartment? You said he was a setter, right?" Jennifer said.

"A pointer."

"Right, one of those. Can I meet him?"

"Sure, he's a sweetheart," I said. I led her into the living room. Jesse stood up in his crate and his tail whipped back and forth. When I opened the door, he wiggled out and pounced on Jennifer, who laughed and caught his paws. She made him 'dance' with her for a moment and then let him back down. Maybe I should consider training him *not* to jump up on guests in the future. Not everyone took it as well as we did when a huge dog was all over them.

"He's beautiful! Such a cute face! I love him!" she said.

"His father spoiled him rotten. I'm not sure I'll be able to keep up with that glamorous lifestyle," I said.

Jennifer giggled and took a seat on the couch. He followed her and she lavished him with even more attention. "Why do you keep him in the crate? Will he scratch up the floors or something?"

I told her about coming home to find my furniture gutted the previous day.

"That's weird. Do you think it's stress?" she said.

I shrugged. "That's all I can think of to explain it."

"Well, I'm sure you can work it out. You know more about dogs than I do," Jennifer said. "I wonder why the family didn't want to adopt him."

"Rick and Mark said he didn't get along with any of them. Taking the dog would bring back too many bad memories, I guess. Oh, well. Their loss," I said.

"Speaking of the boys…" Jennifer's grin spread from ear-to-ear. "Tell me all about them! Are they cuter in real life? Were they scruffy?"

I told her about running into them at the Humane Society and about being invited to the filming on Saturday. And yes, I said they were cuter in real life.

"I asked them if you could come too and they said it would be fine as long as we stayed out of the way."

Jennifer squealed and clapped before hugging me. "You did?! Thank you so much! This is awesome!"

I hugged her back. "It's not a problem. I knew you would want to go."

"Of course! It'll give us the perfect chance to spy on them up close! You'll have all the time you want to drool over Rick," she teased.

I blushed and threw Jesse's stuffed alligator at her.

"I doubt he'll even notice I'm there," I said. "He'll be way too busy."

"He'll notice you if you put yourself out there," Jennifer said. "If you want, I can do some research and find out if he has a girlfriend."

"He doesn't," I replied, maybe too quickly. My cheeks heated up even more. "His Facebook page says he's single. You know that."

"You know that could just be so that he attracts more girls to the series," Jennifer said.

"Doesn't that seem like...I don't know, deception?" I asked.

"It's marketing!" Jennifer said. "Do you think the series would be successful if they didn't have two hot, single guys in the lead rolls? None of the actresses look that bad either. Looks draw in viewers and sometimes it doesn't even matter that they're airheads."

"Well, we know how you get into so many plays now," I said.

It was her turn to throw a squeaky penguin toy at me.

"I'm not ashamed," she said. "I'm going to star in the Chicago Theater one day. But you know, if you married Rick, you wouldn't have to walk another dog ever again."

"I wouldn't mind walking Jesse," I said.

"Well, of course there's him," she replied. "I'm just saying; wouldn't it be nice not have to work another day in your life? The series is free to watch online, but they sell so many DVD's and merchandise. Plus, they get all that money from the ads that play before the videos. He's got to be loaded!"

I thought back to the sleek, black cars the boys had unlocked at the Humane Society. They had to have a good-sized stash of cash at the bank. Now we knew how they could afford all those special effects.

Jennifer was a bit tired from all of her rehearsals and I still wanted to repay her for all the lunches she had made for me that week. I cooked a stew for dinner while we made plans to go to the filming. It was Friday, which meant we would be heading out to find the warehouse the next morning. It was my luck that I had no pet sitting appointments. Jennifer called in sick at the cafe. I made sure that Jesse's crate had enough bedding in it and that he had a couple toys and a bone to keep him occupied.

I would give it another week or two before I left him out during the day to test how well he behaved. When we were hanging out in the evenings, he would often stare out the windows and watch the bustling street below. Mr. Foster's neighborhood had been considerably more posh than mine. The sidewalks of Roger's Park were packed with people and the passing cars on the street kept up a steady drone. It would probably take a while for Jesse to get used to the stream of constant sounds.

Sometimes, I found him sitting and staring hopefully at the front door. It took me a while before I realized that he was waiting for his old master to come back. I wondered, again, if he had any notion that Mr. Foster was gone for good. I couldn't be sure if I felt sorry for him or if I envied him a little bit. Life would be much simpler without having to comprehend death and all it entailed. All Jesse would have to worry about is when he was getting fed next and where to bed down to get the best amount of sunlight.

We took Jennifer's car since I wanted a little break from driving around all the time for work. The warehouse in Oak Park that served as the *Grimoire Danya* studio was forty minutes away. We had to work our way through the tail-end of rush hour traffic to get there. Most people were taking advantage of the sunny day to head to the beach. I had never lived close to water until I lived in Chicago. Now that I had Lake Michigan just a stone's-throw away, I was too busy to visit often. My job was to look after people's pets so that they could either work or go enjoy themselves. In other words, sometimes *I* worked so *they* could go on vacation.

Oak Park was more open and spaced-out than the heart of the city. Stacked condominiums and apartment complexes gave way to divided houses standing side-by-side with green, plush lawns. Eventually, we passed a patch of trees that I recognized from the series and knew we were getting close. They probably had to have special permission from the park district to film there, especially if they wanted to go at night.

Mark had given me the address to the studio just before he left the Humane Society. It was an annex to a restricted factory nestled by the tree line. The factory had worn, ash-tipped smokestacks and broken windows. The warehouse looked cleaner and more modern, having probably been added several years after the factory was built. Running next to the factory was a set of active railroad tracks with strip malls on the other side.

We pulled into an empty spot in the cracked parking lot beside Rick's car. My hand hesitated on the door handle. The thought of meeting the rest of the film-crew was nerve-wracking. Were it not for the fact that Jennifer was already bouncing out of the car, I would have been tempted to turn and head back home.

The entrance was locked, but there was an intercom system on the door frame. I pressed the call button and a chipper voice said, "This is the head office of Weaver Studios. Our management is currently preparing to shoot a scene for the hit series, *Grimoire Danya*. Please state the nature of your visit or leave a message and a callback number. We will get back to you at the next opportunity."

I told the voice my name and said that I had an invitation to the set from Rick Weaver.

"Yes, we were told you were coming, Ms. Gladdis," the secretary said. "I'll unlock the door. Just go straight ahead to the staging area." We heard the latch click and the door opened easily when I pulled it.

"They even have security?" Jennifer whispered to me.

"I'm not surprised," I said. "They must have a lot of good stuff in here."

We went down a bland, white hall and through a set of double doors that led to the warehouse. Half of the interior had been made to look like the inside of a cavern with slimy patches of moss on the rocky walls and Styrofoam stalagmites that hung like unruly rows of teeth.

On the other side of the large room was a raised wooden platform with rickety tables and chairs. There was a long counter with half-filled, bronze tankards and a tall rack of beer kegs.

Set designers were hard at work touching up the details while film techs were checking the cameras and audio equipment. A web of cords stretched over the ground. Everyone else stepped over them with practiced ease while Jennifer and I were hopping around so we didn't step on anything important.

Rick was surrounded by assistants with clipboards who were taking down his every instruction. Once the crowd thinned out, he caught sight of us and waved. I waved back and then felt a little nudge in my ribs from a smirking Jennifer.

"Just look at him in costume! I wish we had better lighting in here so we could see him. Such a cutie!" Jennifer whispered to me. I had to agree. Rick was wearing a long overcoat with dark trousers and leather boots. A scabbard held one of the prop blades around his waist along with several pouches. His stubble had grown out even more over the last couple of days.

"Glad to see you could make it," he said, once he had reached us.

"Thank you so much for letting us watch!" I said. "This is my friend Jennifer. She's another fan of the series."

Jennifer bounded forward to take his hand. "Hey there! This is so exciting! I never thought I would actually get to meet you."

"Thanks. It's always good to know more people like this stuff," Rick said. Underneath his make-up, I could see the lines of exhaustion etched into his face. Was he still dealing with funeral business on top of all of this?

"So what are you filming today?" I said.

"It's a tavern scene for the beginning of the next season," he said. We like to keep everything filmed far in advance. It lets us catch discrepancies, plot holes, that kind of thing. Mark and I do most of the writing while our team helps us edit."

"That must be a lot of work, but you do an amazing job. Is Mark going to be here today?" Jennifer said. She said it casually, but the pink tinge on her cheeks made it obvious she was as excited to see Mark as I had been to see Rick.

"He went to inspect the blades we have in storage. He tries to keep a tight hold on the inventory," Rick said. "The others say he's paranoid, but I think it's a good idea. We don't want to lose anything."

"Do you guys make your own props or buy them?" I said.

Rick unsheathed the sword at his waist and held it out for us to see. "We buy a lot of them from eBay or antique stores. We like to give the weapons an original style, so we do modifications to them."

The sword was thin and the blade gleamed in the light. Someone had sanded the edge so it wasn't sharp.

Better so no one got injured if someone made a mistake in their fighting choreography. The rubies in the hilt looked authentic. I didn't blame Mark for worrying about them.

"That's so cool!" Jennifer said, her eyes wide.

Rick smiled and put the sword back in its sheath. Just then, Mark emerged from a doorway to a back room and came over to us. If we had thought Rick looked good in costume, Mark looked delicious now that we could see him up close. He was wearing a tan shirt buttoned up halfway and his dark hair was tousled. He gave Jennifer and me a curt nod before turning to Rick. "We've got a problem," he muttered.

Rick frowned and said, "Sorry, ladies, can you excuse us for a sec?"

"Sure, we'll be right here," Jennifer said. She hadn't taken her eyes off of Mark once. As the boys hurried to the backroom, I immediately plummeted from Cloud 9 back to Earth. At least Rick seemed friendlier this time around, even if he was still under a lot of stress.

"What do you think they were talking about?" I said, offhandedly.

"I don't know. I wonder if something got stolen," Jennifer said.

"That sounds horrible!" I said. "Can you imagine sinking all that time and money into making a prop, then some jerk comes along and snatches it?"

"I hope they find it again. If they're lucky, it didn't go far." Jennifer said. Her eyes scanned the warehouse.

"Hey, look over there. Isn't that the barmaid from the second season? I thought she was so stale. Why did they bring her back?"

We spent the next ten minutes picking out familiar faces from the crew. Some of the actors with bit parts had been brought back for the tavern scene. I didn't notice Rick and Mark return from storage until I heard Rick's voice thrown over the warehouse with a megaphone.

"All right, everyone! We're getting ready to shoot in fifteen minutes!"

Jennifer gave a little squeal of excitement beside me. "Where do you think they'll want us?" she asked.

An assistant overheard her and pointed to a pair of folding chairs behind the row of cameras. "You two can take seats over there. If you want a drink, there's a break room in the back."

We thanked him and negotiated our way over the cords to the chairs. The extras scurried to their places on the set. Rick and Mark appeared on the wooden platform after everyone else had settled in.

Someone called for silence. Jennifer and I were cast into pitch darkness just before the lights came on over the stage. Rick went over to the cameramen to set up the shots and then took his place at a table. He ran through his lines with Mark a couple times. Dyllas was getting into a heated argument with Averad over the recent assassination of Dyllas's mentor. Finally, Averad smirked and said something that enraged Rick. He sprang to his feet, overturning the table.

"You will not speak of my master in that manner!" he shouted. His face flushed with anger as he glared at Mark, who peered at him shrewdly.

"Your master brought it upon himself. A self-proclaimed expert should have foreseen an ambush at the docks. His fault was his own," Mark said.

"He was going to make things right! He was betrayed!" Rick said. By now, all the other patrons in the 'tavern' were staring at the pair.

"But why would one trying to make amends arrive heavily armed? Maybe he wasn't the man you thought he was," Mark said.

"Shut your mouth! I would lie cold and dead on the ground before I believed your words!" Rick said, unsheathing his sword.

"That can be arranged," Mark said, copying him.

The scene ended and the cameras stopped rolling. Rick went over to the tech crew to discuss more angles. They shot the tavern scene two more times before they called for a break.

"We'll be doing the brawl next, so look over your outfits and make sure nothing is going to break off!" Mark called out.

I heard Rick mutter, "Yeah, we don't need a lawsuit," followed by a chorus of snickers as the extras dispersed.

Jennifer and I were dying to get a word in with the

boys, but they had been surrounded yet again by a make-up artist and supervisors.

"Maybe we should wait until they're done before we talk to them again," I said.

"Well," Jennifer said, with a sly smile. "Since they're busy, why don't we take a look around?"

The idea was tempting. We would probably never have another chance to explore the set, but I didn't want to get in trouble. "What if they don't want us poking around?"

"I'll take care of it," Jennifer said. She went over to a cameraman, giving him her most charming smile. "Excuse me, we were wondering if we could see more of the props?"

The cameraman, a young man with a stocky build and a smattering of freckles on his nose, had already been bewitched. "Is there anything in particular you want to look at?"

"I took a class about medieval studies in college." she said, ignoring me when I covered an incredulous snort with a cough. "I was really impressed with how authentic the outfits looked. It would be great if I could see some of the armor."

The cameraman scratched his head. "We have some spare time now. I can give you a quick tour of the workroom if you want."

"Oh, that would be great! What's your name, anyway?" Jennifer said with a smile that made him blush.

He pulled a key ring out of his pocket. "My name's Brian. Are you coming too?" he said, glancing at me.

I nodded. As long as Jennifer had gotten us in, there was no way I was missing out. As he led us into a workroom, I muttered to Jennifer, "You're a little siren, you know that? And what degree would that class on medieval studies work towards?"

"History, definitely. Maybe Liberal Arts?" She shrugged. "He's kinda cute, isn't he?"

The back room was filled to the brim with swords, crowns, and chain mail. I recognized many of the 'treasures' from the show. There was the Medallion of the South that the king had worn just before he was assassinated. The gold-trimmed shields of the Capital's guardsmen hung in a line on the wall. Some props from the first season were collecting a layer of dust.

"Have you guys ever thought of auctioning this stuff one day?" I asked.

Brian shrugged. "If we do, it'll be up to Rick and Mark. They're the bosses. Whatever they say, goes."

"I know Mark got more involved, but I didn't know he had that much influence," I said. The way Brian was making it sound, Mark had skyrocketed from a bit-actor to a co-director.

"They're business partners now," Brian said. "Once the series started getting popular, Rick needed some help with advertising and sponsors. Mark already had connections since he worked in a few independent films so he was able to help Rick get the sponsorship he needed.

Jennifer pumped her fist behind his back and mouthed, "Score." I rolled my eyes at her. Having a boyfriend with a background like Mark's would help her career go a long way...if she could actually get into a relationship with him, that is.

"Did you help make any props yourself?" I asked.

"I have, actually. When Rick was first starting out, he was really short handed. We were roommates and he only had a few people to help with the weapons and costumes, so I gave him a hand when I could," Brian said.

"Do you have to lock the studio up every night? How many people know you guys use this warehouse?" I said.

Brian shifted his feet uncomfortably. "Well, we try not to make it known to the general public, even during the interviews. If we did, we might have a big crowd outside every day."

"Right, don't worry about us. We won't go blabbing anywhere," I said.

He smiled a bit at me. "Right, thanks." He glanced at the rack where the swords were mounted. "Just between us, we've been having a little trouble with our stock. Last week, someone managed to get in here and make off with one of the silver knives."

In the back of my mind, I wondered if this had something to do with whatever Mark had had to discuss with Rick when we saw them go to the back rooms earlier. I felt like snooping a little more. "Doesn't the studio have pretty good security?"

"We have security guards who patrol at all times," Brian said. "None of them saw anything. We even checked the security cameras for the evening we think the knife was stolen. There's no sign of anyone breaking in."

"That's so bizarre. Are there any fire escapes the thief may have used?" I said. I had wondered the same thing about James Foster's killer. "It was just the knife that was stolen, right?"

"Yeah, it was just that one knife, which is weird, considering how much other stuff they could have taken as well. All of the emergency exits have an alarm. Somebody would have noticed if they were opened." Brian paused for a moment. "Honestly, I think whoever it was had a key to the building, but there were only five keys made. Rick and Mark have two and each of the managers have one. Rick and Mark entered the building once, but that was so Rick could get a knife to get refurbished. I think their Uncle owns a weapons shop somewhere in town. Everyone else who checked in during that time was either here for the costumes or to work on the set." He chose a particular key off of his key ring and presented it to us proudly. "I've got a key, too, since I need to come in every other night to check the camera equipment, but I was out of town last week, so I wasn't around when everything happened."

"Don't worry, we believe you," I said. "Has anyone called the police yet?"

"Yeah, they came the day after the knife was reported missing. There aren't many leads, though. The police said they would tell us if they found anything, but other than that, we're on our own."

"I see," I said, briefly. Truth be told, I didn't want to dwell too much on the subject. Discussing the police just made me remember my own uncomfortable dealings with them back in the lobby of Mr. Foster's apartment building. Which, in turn, brought my thoughts back to Mr. Foster. I tried to cheer myself up by thinking of Jesse instead. He must be getting so bored in his crate. I would take him to the park that evening and let him stretch his legs.

"Whoever took it knew what they were after. It was the only piece missing and it had gems in it that make it pretty valuable. We've already searched the studio pretty extensively in case it was just misplaced and we couldn't find it anywhere. We'll just need to tighten up security around here so no one tries to steal anything again," Brian said.

"We'll cross our fingers that you find the knife again," Jennifer said.

"Thanks. All right, if you guys are done, we should probably be heading back out. We're almost done with the break," Brian said.

He locked the door to the workroom once we left and slipped the key back into his pocket. He seemed like a nice guy; one who genuinely cared about *Grimoire Danya*. I didn't think he would have stolen the knife, but I was having a hard time trusting my impressions of people as of late. First, I had thought Mr. Foster was too kind and amiable to have bad blood with anyone, much less his family. Then Mark and Rick, who always seemed like nice guys on TV, had been so uncaring towards their grandfather's death. For all I knew, Brian was swiping knives all the time and pawning them off!

The actors returned to the set and Jennifer and I took our places on the folding chairs. The make-up artists had added smudges to Rick and Mark's faces. They were wearing more tattered versions of their costumes. I heard Jennifer murmur "yummy," when she saw the slashes in Mark's white, billowy shirt.

Rick had had similar rips in his overcoat, but it was a replica of the original, which hung up on a nearby rack, still in perfect condition. They must have had multiple versions for some scenes.

The lights dimmed and silence was called for. Rick and Mark rehearsed a few more lines and reviewed the choreography for the fight scene, giving instructions to the extras when needed. Rick was very particular about the sword fighting. He had mentioned in an interview that he had taken some fencing classes for the sake of accuracy.

They shot every scene up to four times, resetting everything every time the cameras stopped recording. After they were done with the fourth session, an assistant appeared on stage and whispered something to Rick, who grimaced. He told everyone to take a ten-minute break and then said a few words to Mark before disappearing off-stage.

"What do you think is going on?" Jennifer said to me.

"No idea, but Mark looks worried," I said.

I watched Rick's progress through the room. After my eyes adjusted to the darkness outside the stage lights, I nearly gasped when I recognized the two figures Rick was approaching. Those detectives, Neal and Carl, were here.

Chapter 7

It had been a few days since I had last seen them and I wasn't sure I liked their sudden appearance. Why were they here of all places? Was it something to do with Mr. Foster's case? I pointed them out to Jennifer. "Those are the detectives who questioned me about the murder last Sunday."

"You're kidding me. Any idea why they're here?" she said. When I shook my head, she asked, "Well, are you going to sit there or are you going to find out? I totally would."

"I can't just walk up and ask them. That stuff is confidential!" I said.

"No, but you can listen in! For crap's sake, haven't you seen any crime shows? Or read *Harriet the Spy*? There's nothing wrong with a little eavesdropping now and then," she said. "Besides, you were the one who found the body! You deserve to know this stuff!"

I was pretty sure there was a difference between casual eavesdropping and listening in on a conversation between a detective and a potential witness. Despite my reservations, curiosity won me over, as it usually did. "Alright. If anyone asks, tell them I'm in the bathroom," I said, glancing at Brian, who was working on a camera a few feet away.

The rest of the crew was going to a nearby lounge for their break. I didn't bump into anyone as I made my way over to where the detectives were talking with Rick. A couple of thick wires almost tripped me, but I managed to save myself before I drew too much attention. I crept along the wall until I could hide behind a pair of heavy, stacked black trunks. I tried to tune out every other sound but their voices. From the sounds of things, I had come in during the middle of their conversation.

"...don't care if I stay in costume. We've still got a lot of filming to get done," Rick said to the detectives.

"Not at all," Detective Carl said, "We're just going to ask you a couple of questions about James and we'll be on our way."

"There's not much I could tell you about him. Can't you talk to my mother? She knew him way better than I did. I hadn't heard from him in years, actually," Rick said, sounding bitter.

"We've already contacted Marietta," Carl said. "She's been able to give us a lot of information. She mentioned that James backed your web series with quite a bit of money two years ago."

"Yes, he did. It's just about the only thing he did to help me out," Rick said. "He sent us a check in the mail with a note saying he wished us luck. That's all the interaction we had."

"Weren't you happy with the sum?" Neal said.

"Look, I'm not saying I was ungrateful for the money," Rick said. "But honestly, he hasn't done a thing to acknowledge my existence since then. It felt like he was just trying to get his name in the credits. My family provides enough funding for everything we need so it's not like we really needed his donation. I would have appreciated it more if he had asked what the series was about. Shown some interest. I doubt he ever watched an episode. What was he trying to pull?"

"I see. Are you sure that's the last contact you had with him?" Carl said.

"I'm sure. I can't think of anything else," Rick said.

"Can you tell us why communications between him and your family were so strained?" Neal said.

Rick scoffed. "The man was a manipulative bastard. That's all you need to know."

I couldn't believe my ears. Was Rick really talking about the same guy that I had visited just about every other day for the past six months? James Foster had never seemed manipulative to me. He was just an eccentric, lonely, old man who loved his dog and hated hot weather. I never thought Rick would be the kind of person who could talk about anyone like this, either.

"I'll ask you to use more respectful language when discussing the recently deceased," Carl said.

Rick held up his hands in apology. "Sorry, sorry. It's just a sore spot with everyone."

"We also read that you've had trouble with people trespassing in your studio?" Neal said.

Here, Rick hesitated before saying, "Yeah, it's really not that big a deal. We called the police and they're still looking."

"Nothing has come up yet?" Neal said.

"Not yet. Why, have you got something?"

"No, do you think you might be able to give us a description of the knife?"

"One-and-a-half inches from edge to spine with a length of six inches," Rick said. I peeked out from behind the trunk to see Rick measuring the dimensions with his hands as he explained. "Silver blade and the handle is made of foam with a wood core. We painted it to make it look older."

"Was it sharpened?" Neal asked.

"No," Rick said, a little abruptly. "We keep all of them dull for safety reasons. If you'll wait for a second, I can see if Mark has a picture of the knife to show you."

"If he could, we would be much obliged," Carl said.

While Rick went off to get Mark, I headed back through the shadows to my chair beside Jennifer. It didn't look as though anyone had bothered her about where I had gone. The actors and tech crew were coming back from their break and heading towards the stage. Jennifer leaned over to me when I was settled in.

"Well? Did they say anything important?" she whispered.

My mind was still trying to process everything I had heard. I glanced around the room. I could probably talk about it here without anybody overhearing, but I was feeling inexplicably on edge, like there were eyes watching from the darkness outside of the stage.

"I'll tell you in the car," I said, keeping my eyes on a group of men overturning the chairs. I didn't want to tell her how Rick had sounded talking about James like he was a revolting hermit. Let her live with a good impression of him just a little bit longer while we were here.

Jennifer pouted and would have bugged me to tell her everything if Rick hadn't chosen that moment to stride back on the stage and call out that they were about to resume filming. The detectives must have left. The rest of the day went on without another hitch. Recording action sequences required a lot more planning than I realized. While most of the shots were focused on Dyllas and Averad, the extras were on the move as well and Rick was constantly rechecking the cameras. He had gotten over the shock of the detective's visit rather fast. The fight ended with Dyllas disarmed and on the ground, with the tip of

Averad's sword pointed underneath his chin.

"Like master, like student. You still have a lot to learn," Averad said.

Dyllas glared up at him. "You've played cat-and-mouse with me long enough. Why don't you finish the job? It would make things much easier for you."

Averad laughed, though his eyes gleamed (I heard a tiny squeal from Jennifer). "I could, but I have a feeling we'll need help from each other again before too long. Shame to let all we've worked for go to waste. Take care."

He strode towards the door in back of the stage without offering a hand to Dyllas, who was picking himself off the ground. Once Rick made sure he was satisfied with the shot, everyone was dismissed.

Jennifer wanted to take pictures with the guys in their costumes, but they were swamped with stagehands again and would probably want to get dressed in regular clothes as soon as business was done. When we saw the tech crew pack away their equipment, we took it as our cue to leave.

I stopped us at the door to the white hallway when I remembered what Mark had said about bringing the supplies for Jesse from Mr. Foster's apartment. Mark appeared nearby after a long moment, heading towards the doorway. His make-up had been removed and he was dressed in jeans and a t-shirt. His scruff was still there, but that was all that remained of Averad.

"I'm glad I caught you before you went back

home! I've got the things for the dog in the back of my truck," he said.

"Oh, great! It's a big help, believe me," I said. "Is Rick still changing?"

"Yeah, he'll take a bit longer. He's got more wounds to clean off than I did," Mark said. It could have been my imagination, but I thought his smile turned smug. "We use latex for the injuries. I don't know how it doesn't bother him. It makes me itch like crazy."

To my surprise, he led us to a navy blue pick-up truck rather than the sleek number he had driven at the Humane Society. He dragged a box off the back that had been labeled "Dog" with black marker.

"Where are you parked? I can take this to your car," he said to me.

"You don't have to do that! I can take care of it," I said.

"It's no big deal. I'm just sorry we didn't get to talk with you a bit more. Did you like the show?" he said.

"It was awesome! You have no idea..." Jennifer said. She only took her eyes off Mark long enough to unlock the trunk of her car and move aside some emergency supplies. Mark put the box in once the space was cleared.

"That's good. I keep telling Rick we should give tours of the studio once in a while, but then we get too busy," he said, closing the lid.

I fidgeted, wondering if I should ask this question or not, but I wanted to get Mark's take on the situation. "I did notice that some detectives came by, though. What did they want to talk about?"

Mark's grin faded. "You noticed that, huh? They were all right. They just wanted to ask Rick about our inventory. Nothing big."

I nodded casually. I didn't want to give away just how much I had overheard. "Well, that's good. Actually, they were the same detectives who questioned me about James Foster. That's the only reason why I asked."

"Really?" Mark said. "I guess I shouldn't be surprised. They didn't stress you out too much, did they?"

"No," I said, though I was surprised. It wasn't lost on me that this was Mark Bishop asking after my welfare. I almost blushed at all the attention. Hopefully, Jennifer wasn't going to be jealous. "They were nice about it, at least."

"I'll bet. Cross your fingers that they won't need to bother you anymore," Mark said. "Actually, I wanted to let you know that the funeral services for grandfather are going to be tomorrow afternoon if you want to come..."

"Oh, sure..." I said, the heat draining from my face. "I'd like to come. It'd be nice to see him off."

Mark smiled only halfway and gave me the address to the funeral home. Then he said, "Well, I have to go and help finish up. I'll talk to you later, alright?"

We waved him off and I leaned against the side of

my car. The sun-heated surface felt as though it was burning through my shirt, but I didn't care. I felt more winded than if I had finished an hour-long walk with a full-grown Boxer.

"I think he was into you," Jennifer told me once Mark was out of earshot.

"W-what makes you say that?" I asked. This time, I must have turned beet red because Jennifer giggled.

"Are you kidding me? I've read tons of relationship columns, April. I know the signs," she said.

I groaned. "You can't be serious. You know those are all crap written for desperate teenagers, right?"

"There's always a kernel of truth, though! He barely noticed me that whole time! And he actually sounded sincere when he asked if those detectives had been nice to you," she said.

"He was being polite, that's all!" I said. I couldn't afford to hope for anything more, so I tried to convince myself of that. All they had offered was to let us come out and watch the shoot, nothing more and nothing less. Mark hadn't asked for my phone number or anything, so I doubted he was actually interested. Both he and Rick had more important things to worry about than a lowly dog walker from the Illinois cornfields.

I told Jennifer everything I had heard between Rick and the detectives on the drive back to Roger's Park. She didn't have much to say about the knife being stolen, but she was astonished by how Rick had been acting.

"That's so weird...He didn't seem cranky or anything when we were talking to him," she said. "He's probably been dealing with the police a lot. I know that would make me cranky if I had to deal with my jobs on top of that and everything else."

"I know. I just can't figure out what could have happened," I said. "I'm not close to some of my aunts and uncles, but I'm not calling them heartless bastards."

"Well, the guy could have paid their web series more attention. I know if I had a celebrity relative, I would be talking to them every chance I got! And not always just to ask for money, I promise!" Jennifer said.

I rolled my eyes and let the subject drop. We weren't going to get anywhere throwing theories around. We spent the majority of the drive chatting about our favorite moments from the fight scene until we pulled up in front of our building. She helped me lift the box from her trunk and get it up to my apartment. Jesse whimpered and shuffled his paws, wriggling around excitedly. We set the box next to the coffee table and I thanked Jennifer for her help. She couldn't stick around as she was going to dinner with some other people from her theater group. I would have invited her to come with me to James's funeral the next day, but she had rehearsal. I was going to have to brave that alone.

"If you see the boys there, you should give them a hug. You know, to comfort them!" she said, with a wink. I blushed and rolled my eyes, which just made her giggle again. I would probably just pay my respects and then hide in the back row of the funeral home for the rest of the ceremony.

When she left, I went over to Jesse's crate and opened the latch on his door. He bolted out and licked my hand in greeting. He sniffed the box curiously while I used a knife to open it up. The trove inside consisted of bags of food, bowls, and toys – both squeaky and stuffed – wedged into whatever free spaces there were. There was an extra dog bed that I stored in the hall closet. It would be a good spare if Jesse tore up the one he was using now.

He was currently having a tearful reunion with his favorite toys. There was a rubber dog bone that must have squeaked once until Jesse broke it. He brought it over and looked up at me expectantly. I glanced over at the box. I still had to unpack the rest of it, but I decided I could deal with that later and placed it on top of the dog bed in the closet.

For the rest of the evening, I wound up settling down on the couch with the TV on, throwing the bone across the room for him to bring back. Fascinating how dogs could never get tired of the endless cycle of fetch. Whatever made Jesse happy made me happy – a quote that would probably be tattooed on my butt before the week was up.

Chapter 8

When I woke up the next morning, there was a dog's nose in my face. I had just enough time to open my eyes before Jesse sneezed and snot splattered across my cheek. There was much groaning and cursing while I ran to the bathroom to wash my face. I went to the kitchen and Jesse was panting happily next to his food bowl, none-the-wiser.

The funeral was at one, so I had plenty of time to get ready. I spent most of it trying to decide what to wear. Like I said, I don't dress for beauty when I'm out walking dogs. Over the past six months, whatever fashion sense my mother had tried to plant in me had shriveled up.

I was caught between finding something appropriate for a funeral yet not wanting to look like a professional mourner in front of the Grimoire boys. I settled on a short-sleeved, black dress with one of the only pairs of heels I had. Thank goodness walking in heels was something you didn't forget, kind of like riding a bicycle.

I waited to put Jesse back in his crate until the very last minute, when I had my purse and keys in my hand. This time, all it took to coax him inside was a treat. Some dogs would resist going back into their crates if they didn't want to be cooped up all day. That Jesse wasn't fighting back was a good sign.

My GPS took me way up towards the northern border of Evanston. The sky was full of gray clouds and the humidity clung to my skin. While I would have been happy for some rain to get rid of the humidity, I hoped it waited until after they put the body in the ground. Was it too soon for a thought like that? I suddenly felt self-conscious. I was still having a hard time thinking of James Foster as being *dead*, even after a week. I was still expecting another day when I would have to stride up to his fancy apartment and see him enjoying his air conditioning and 54-inch TV. The feeling would probably fade over time. At least, I hoped it would.

The funeral home was a one-story, stone building with its own parking lot (hallelujah!) and a small garage in the side for the hearses. The sign out in front announced the services for 'James Foster, March 21, 1940- July 15, 2012.' There was a good handful of other cars, but the parking lot wasn't packed. I saw Rick's and Mark's cars among them.

With a breath to gather my courage, I headed up the short walkway. The entrance hall had an usher who asked me if I was here to pay my respects to Mr. Foster. He showed me into the viewing room, which was serene with floral carpeting and bouquets in vases. There were four rows of lightly cushioned chairs with an aisle leading up to the coffin at the head of the room. Everything was clean and there was a hint of lavender blossom perfume to the air. My nerves calmed a tad.

Most of those attending were already seated, but there was a small line leading up next to the coffin, which had the upper half of its lid opened. I stood in the back of the line and peered around. Rick and Mark were talking in the doorway to another room. They were dressed in dark suits and had shaved since they had filmed for the series yesterday. Amazing what a difference a day could make in an actor.

The boys were dry-eyed, but so were most of the other attendants. Even if Mr. Foster apparently hadn't been well-loved, there were more people than I had expected. Jennifer would have said they might just feel obligated to come. I really hoped I wasn't the only person who sincerely missed him.

Within moments, I stood beside the coffin. It was made of a dark walnut wood with a bed of satin pillows. Laying there, with his eyes closed and his hands propped up on his belly, was James Foster. He wore an off-white suit and his gray hair had been neatly combed. His skin looked paler, almost like plaster. But other than that, it was him. As eerie as this was, I preferred it to seeing him slouched over in his own blood.

Maybe it was weird for me to keep staring at him. I didn't cry. I missed him, of course. I wished this hadn't happened, but I didn't cry. Should I have felt guilty for that?

I felt a slender hand on my arm and turned my head automatically. Smiling at me was a middle-aged woman with long, brown hair, green eyes, and features that could have been lifted from Rick's face except they were more angled and proud. Her black dress-suit and head scarf were considerably heavier than I would have dared to wear in the middle of summer. The scarf allowed for a thin, black veil over her face.

"Excuse me, dear. Are you the dog walker that found my father?" she asked. Her voice had a low, delicate quality to it, like a sleeping cat's purr. I nodded at her question and she held out a gloved hand for me to shake. "Marietta Weaver. What is your name?"

"April Gladdis. It's nice to meet you," I said. "All of us at the company are very sorry for your loss." Cheryl had wanted to attend the funeral, but she hadn't been able to clear her schedule. I was technically a representative of the company as well as myself.

"I'm getting to the age where I see more family and friends departing than I would like," she said. "I thought I would be used to it by now, but father took me by surprise. It must have been terrible for you. How are you doing?"

I didn't quite know how to respond to that. I had felt normal for the past week up until now. "It just feels...weird, to think that he's gone. He was very nice when I spoke to him."

"Ah, so you did see him often?" she said.

"He hired us to walk his dog every weekday. I was the one assigned to him," I said. "I saw him at noon and sometimes in the evening. We usually had a little chance to talk," I said.

"How sweet," she said. Her dreamy smile hadn't grown or faltered in all the time we were talking. "I do want to talk to you about him. I regret to say I didn't have a proper conversation with him for the last five years. You knew him better in his last days than I did."

There was something about this that should have made me feel uncomfortable, but it all felt so surreal that I didn't feel anxious or awkward at all. "He treated me well. He even offered me a glass of water on the hot days. I could tell Jesse loved him a lot, too."

"Jesse was the star of his life. I'm glad he had someone to keep him company. I'm sure it meant so much to him that you took such good care of his dog," Marietta said. "My son told me you adopted him."

"Yeah. He's pretty well settled, now," I said.

"Good to hear. Well, if you will excuse me, I must talk to the funeral director. Will you be coming with us to the cemetery?" she asked, to which I said yes. "Then you must come find me after it's over. I want to hear more."

She headed off in the direction of the doorway where Rick and Mark had been. I glanced at Mr. Foster one more time before going to sit down in the back.

The service wasn't long. Mark gave the eulogy and an old business partner gave a few words for the departed.

At the end, the casket was closed and a group of men, Rick and Mark included, carried it into the garage. The cemetery was located three blocks away. I followed the slow train of cars until we arrived inside the gates. The cemetery was private and well-funded, from the looks of all the trees and the elaborate headstones. The sky still promised rain, but it seemed to be holding off. We followed the casket to the freshly dug plot and watched in silence as it was lowered in.

I glanced around at everyone gathered. Mark was standing next to Marietta but Rick was nowhere to be found. He must have gone already. It seemed a bit insensitive to me, but I didn't know if there was a good reason behind it. I would give Rick the benefit of the doubt.

As the casket was slowly covered, the crowd began to disperse and head back to their cars. I went over to Marietta to see if she still wanted to talk. Mark was still nearby. When he saw me coming closer, he smiled.

"Hey, you wound up coming after all. My mother just told me she spoke with you already," he said.

That caught me by surprise. Had Mark just called Marietta his mother? If they were related, did that mean Mark and Rick were related as well? They didn't have the same last name and they didn't really look alike, but they could have been half-brothers for all I knew. None of the *Grimoire Danya* fan sites I visited regularly ever said anything about this. Even Facebook had them listed as friends, but not family.

"I was here for the viewing too. I was just sitting in the back," I said.

"I'm sure he would have been glad to see you here," Mark said. He looked grimly at the filling grave. "The investigation's still going on, even if they're done with the body."

Marietta sighed. "The police were asking so many questions yesterday. I'm tired of it. Do you have time, April? I still want to ask you about my father."

"Yes, I do. What do you want to know?" I said. Honestly, I had no idea what I would be able to tell her. I could count the number of times James had spoken about his personal life on one hand.

"Did he seem happy? Was he ever angry or stressed?" she asked. "He was such a stubborn man. If he was frustrated, he would make sure everyone knew it."

"I didn't think he was unhappy," I replied. "He liked to watch the news a lot and he was really chatty when I went to walk Jesse. Sometimes he looked tired, but I figured it was for health reasons, you know?"

"I see. He must have been very fond of you," Marietta said. "Did he ever tell you about his family?"

"Not really. In fact, I didn't even know Rick and Mark were related to him. I only found out when they told me," I said. "Didn't he know about *Grimoire Danya*?"

Mark nodded. "He did, but he wasn't interested in fantasy. Thought it was a waste of time when we're supposed to be living in the real world, I guess. He didn't like filling his head with anything that wasn't business."

"It just wasn't the kind of thing he liked to watch, Mark. Don't be offended by it," Marietta said to him.

"I'm not offended," Mark said, though it sounded a bit quick to me. "We've always had a bunch of viewers, no matter what he thought."

"I'm sure he would have liked it if he had given it a chance. He must have known how hard you guys worked on it," I said, trying to sound reassuring.

"It's a shame he didn't take more of an interest in us. He and I used to be so close, even after my mother died. It was him, my brothers, and me," Marietta said, her eyes taking on a faraway look. "Those were happier times. Other families in our particular situation always seemed to stay together out of obligation. I always felt we were closer and not just because of our blood. I would have liked it to stay that way...but then my younger brother died and things started to fall apart. There was nothing I could do to stop it."

Mark frowned. "I don't think April cares about all that, mother."

"No! It's fine," I said, quickly. I wanted to know more about what their 'particular situation' had entailed, but decided it would be prying too deeply if she didn't want to share. "I'm sorry about your brother."

It was the first time that serene smile on Marietta's face faded away. "Derek's death was even more sudden than my father's. None of us were expecting it. He was only twenty-two, the same age as Mark, actually." Mark looked away, but Marietta continued. "He was shot in the crossfire of a gang shooting, the poor thing. It's shameful, really. This November will be the twenty-fifth anniversary of his death."

"That sounds awful. I'm very sorry I brought it up," I said, grimacing.

"Don't trouble yourself over it," she said. "I just...can't help but think that they died in the same way, because of an act of senseless violence. Derek was shot and now, years later, my father was stabbed. Like son, like father, dying by the hands of man."

"It's a coincidence," Mark said, shrugging. "I wouldn't think about it too hard."

"I'm afraid he never mentioned anything about Derek to me," I said.

"It affected him, I know, but he would never have admitted it. It split us up, put distance between us. The gap just...grew and grew. We spoke to each other less, until it was years before I heard from him," she said.

"Was he the same with your other brother you mentioned? If you don't mind me asking, I mean," I said.

"Yes, as far as I know. His name is Jim We all called him 'Jim' when we were little. Oh, that was so long ago." She dabbed at her eyes with a handkerchief from her purse. "His friends like to call him that still, every now and then. If you're lucky enough that he calls you 'friend,' that is," she said.

"Or unlucky enough," Mark muttered, earning him a blank look from his mother. He shrugged. "Well, he didn't show up today. I wouldn't call him much of a friend."

For the first time, Marietta's eyes turned cold. "Yes, I suppose you are right about that. It's strange that I should be the one with the courage to show my face and say goodbye. And after all his talk of being the last one to stay completely loyal to father."

"If you ask me, I think he just didn't want to have to look us in the eyes, for all the trouble he caused us. Now his main supporter is gone, after all," Mark said. The look that Marietta gave him said that the subject was closed.

"Look at us talking about all this trivial family business in front of you, April. You should go home before you get caught in the downpour. Besides, you must stay very busy," she said. "Thank you for indulging my curiosity."

"It's no problem," I said, smiling. What did I have to get back to, again? Right, a night of Jesse, going to the dog park, and maybe a bit of reading or TV before bed. It sure sounded riveting. Having a day off still felt weird when I spent the rest of my time rushing around.

"Have a safe drive home. I hope your dogs are good for you," Marietta said.

I said goodbye and started heading back to my car. When I was about at the halfway point, I heard Mark calling my name and turned to see him coming after me at a light jog. I turned to meet him.

"I was kicking myself for not asking about this yesterday," he said, dragging his fingers through his dark hair, maybe a little nervously. "I wanted to get your phone number, if you're okay with it."

When I heard that, my stomach did a massive flop and all the serenity from the afternoon scurried away to cower in the corner. This was real, right? I wasn't dreaming? "Um...y-yeah! Sure!"

"Thanks, it's just that with all the police stuff that's going on...I thought it would be nice to know someone from the outside who knows what actually happened. Hell, you were there," Mark said.

I just nodded, my mouth agape. I hoped he didn't care that I probably looked like a fish. This was better than I could have imagined in a million years. Mark was actually inviting me to be a friend! Or...something like that. A confidant? A secret buddy? I don't know, but I was getting his phone number!

We swapped numbers and he said, "Thanks. I was worried you'd think it was awkward or something. Everyone I know is either with the show already or interested in business...or a fan." He chuckled.

"Not at all! You can message me anytime. I swear it's not a problem," I said. "If there's any way I can help, I'm happy to do it!"

We said goodbye and I watched him go back to Marietta. I drove back home in a daze, hoping I hadn't sounded too much like a child who had been told they were going to Disney. Drops of water began splashing on the windshield, but a monsoon could have broken over me for all I cared. I had Mark's phone number. Maybe I would even get Rick's eventually. Jennifer would freak when she heard about this.

It rained on and off for a couple hours after I got home, but Jesse and I had a window of sunlight to go outside after dinner. It had occurred to me during our walks that he must not have had much opportunity to socialize with other dogs since he had been staying home with Mr. Foster all day. Due to company policy, we were supposed to keep the dogs we were walking away from other dogs and people, even going so far as to cross the street if we saw them coming. Our dog could have the sweetest personality in the world, but you wouldn't know if the other dog was aggressive until the dogs had their jaws fastened around each other. That would be very difficult to tell a client.

Jesse had never lunged at other dogs, though. He was prone to watching them curiously. He would whimper and pull a bit when he saw one that he wanted to meet, but he wasn't going to bolt and yank the leash out of my hand like some others. I had located a dog park a few blocks away from my apartment. It might be worth it to take him there and see how he did with the other dogs. When I saw that the rain had stopped, I hooked on Jesse's harness and set off to find it again.

One of the advantages dogs have over humans is that the process for meeting strangers is faster and involves less awkward small talk. A dog would meet a new dog, sniff his or her butt, and would then know the equivalent to a human's daily schedule and family tree. Within fifteen minutes of being at the dog park, Jesse had gone off with a Lhasa apso and a Dalmatian for a game of soccer.

It was pretty easy for dog owners to get acquainted with each other too, once the dogs were occupied. Sometimes I would try and guess which owners belong to which dog before I met them. The Lhasa apso, for example, belonged to a middle-aged businessman who commuted to the Loop every morning while the Dalmatian was owned by a couple who said they had three cats in their condominium as well. I had always wanted to have both a dog and a cat (three might be too much for me). Now I was halfway there.

The dog park was fenced in between two apartment buildings and had play areas made of wood-fiber and grass. There were trash bins by every entrance with free poop bag containers hanging above them. Most of the owners were pretty conscientious about picking up after their dogs. It was more obvious here who wasn't doing their duty than it would be on a sidewalk. It was shocking how many neighborhoods just didn't care, to the point where there were piles of fossilized dog waste every few feet.

My company made it mandatory to pick up after the dogs, but I would have done it without the rule. I had more common courtesy than to let the dogs go wherever they wanted and just leave it there. I was cleaning up after

Jesse in the grass when I happened to look up at a German shepherd sitting a few feet away and saw a silver cylinder on her collar.

    I gasped and took another look around. There were five dogs at the park besides Jesse. Three of them had silver cylinders. Maybe I should have made Jesse wear his so he could be trendy. I had taken it off when he started living with me and put it on my bookshelf so I wouldn't lose it. Out of curiosity, I asked the man with the Lhasa apso what they were for, seeing as his dog had a cylinder. He laughed and said they were for ID tags. I guess that settled it, then, but it still puzzled me that not even the workers at the Humane Society had known what they were for.

    I threw tennis balls for Jesse and his friends to chase, amazed by how much energy Jesse actually had stored up. After about an hour and a half, dusk was settling in. I put Jesse's leash back on and looked over to say goodbye to the couple from before when I noticed that they were taking the silver cylinder off of the German shepherd and putting it on the Dalmatian's collar. Now that was odd. I thought they were supposed to be used to identify dogs. Why were they placing the ID tag on a different dog?

    When we had returned home, I found Jesse's cylinder and attached it to his collar. If it was a trend, I wanted him to be stylish! It would also remind me to see about tracking down a chip to place inside. As assured as I was that Jesse would never purposefully bolt away from me and get lost, I would be the first person to admit that crazy things were prone to happen at the most unexpected times. It never hurt to be too careful.

I got a call from Jennifer asking me if I had stolen any hugs at the funeral. I told her that, while I hadn't gotten a hug, I had been able to get Mark's phone number. Jennifer let out a squeal that would have split my ear drums if I hadn't held the phone away from my face.

"Well? Have you called them?" she said.

"What am I going to say? I missed you even though it's only been six hours?" I said.

"Ask them if they've had the chance to edit what they filmed yesterday," she said.

"Maybe...I don't want to seem like I'm nagging them to come out with new stuff every day," I said.

"Then ask them if they've found their missing knife!"

"We're not supposed to know about that! It was a cameraman that took us back there and I had to listen in on Rick's conversation with the detectives to know the details!" I said.

"You're so hopeless!" she said, exasperated.

"I'm trying not to smother them!" I said, though I could hear her laughing over the phone.

As it turned out, I didn't have to be the one to initiate a conversation with the boys. A bit later, Mark sent me a text to thank me again for going to the funeral. Apparently, our talk had cheered up Marietta considerably, considering she and Rick seemed to be fighting a lot nowadays.

When I asked him if they got the chance to see her often, he replied, Not as much as you'd think, since we've been working on the series so much. We visited her some last week and were there when she heard about grandpa.

Well, at least they had been together to hear the news. Although, they probably hadn't been driven into mourning when they did find out. They only seemed mildly inconvenienced by his passing, now. It was hard for someone like me to comprehend, when my own grandparents had been a couple towns away and we would visit them every other week to get spoiled rotten. The ones on my father's side had passed away when I was too young to really know them, but my mother's parents had taken every opportunity to shower Toby and me with candy and presents, even taking us to their cabin in northern Wisconsin during the summer. They were both still with us today, though this entire episode had given me a new appreciation for that fact. It was easy for me as a child to think that everyone in my family would be with me forever, but I had seen first hand how quickly things could change. If something were to happen to either of them, or any of my family for that matter, I don't think I would ever be able to stop crying. I definitely wouldn't handle it with the same aloof and disdainful attitude as Mr. Foster's family.

Mark and I didn't message each other much longer after that, just a few words about the weather and a wish for a good day tomorrow. A brief conversation and one that I definitely enjoyed a lot more than I should have. I unloaded more of Jesse's supplies from the box, finding enough toys for four dogs. Jesse picked up a number of them, shook them around, and then settled in the corner to work on a terry cloth cube. I kept pulling things out until my hand hit something hard and wooden. It was a black picture frame, similar to the one I remembered above Mr. Foster's electrical fireplace. I must have passed by it dozens of times. It held a picture of Jesse, with his head tilted and eyes wide, looking innocently up at the camera.

  Maybe Mark had included the picture in with the box since I was the one who had taken Jesse. That was awfully thoughtful of him...I felt warmth rise to my cheeks and chided myself. Mustn't get my hopes up too much. I set it on the coffee table and looked up at Jesse, who scurried over to me and dropped a squeaky ball at my feet. I tried to swap it out with a stuffed rabbit, mindful that the squeaker might disturb one of the neighbors at this hour. He was hesitant to give up on the ball, but the second the rabbit soared across the room, he forgot all about the ball.

  We didn't keep it up for long. Hearing the way his paws trampled across the hardwood floor like a herd of horses made me worry for the people downstairs. I had a pretty early start tomorrow, anyway. Cheryl had asked if I could fill-in for another sitter who was taking care of a diabetic cat in remission. He needed to be fed every twelve hours and the morning feeding was earlier than I was used to. If I didn't get enough sleep, I might ignore my alarm clock when it went off. As much as I hated to do it, I should put Jesse in his crate for tonight so that his moving around in the bed wouldn't disturb me. I would let him out first thing in the morning.

I threw the rabbit one more time, but the trajectory was thrown off by a huge yawn, sending it bouncing off the wall rather than down the hall. Jesse bumped into the coffee table in his haste to get the toy. I could only watch helplessly as the picture of Jesse wobbled threateningly and then tilted off the edge. I made a desperate lunge to grab it, but it still hit the floor. Of course, it had to land on the glass side, too. There was a sickening shatter and I froze. Jesse winced and turned to stare at me and the glass bits on the floor.

With a sinking feeling, I picked up the frame. I would have to sweep up the shards before either Jesse or I stepped on them by accident. Over Jesse's face was a spider web of cracks. It was enough damage to warrant getting a new frame. At least the picture was safe.

I prodded around the back and found the latch for the flap that kept the picture in. I opened it up to find that Jesse's picture was not the only thing in the frame. Tucked in between the picture and the cardboard backing was another photo and a piece of yellowing newsprint.

The photo was of a seated young woman with two men standing on either side of her. I took a closer look at the woman, who, for some reason, looked familiar to me. My eyes scanned over her dark brown hair, green eyes, and angled facial features. The picture was a tad grainy, having been taken years previously, but those faces were clear.

All at once, it clicked. The woman was Marietta as a teenager! Following that logic, the young men with her must be her brothers. The taller man I guessed was the oldest and the shorter boy, her younger brother. I wracked my brain to remember the names. Marietta had mentioned her older brother had been Jim while the younger had been named...Derek, that's right. And Derek was the one who had passed away.

It was weird, looking at them now. They looked happy – or at least their smiles looked sincere, unlike those fake smiles that people wore in Christmas photos when they didn't like the ones right beside them. Derek couldn't have been more than fifteen here. Considering that he had been Mark's age when he died (and therefore, a year younger than me), he would have only had seven more years to live after the picture was taken. He and Jim were just about polar opposites in appearance. Derek's face had a round, boyish quality to it while Jim had a strong jaw and sharp eyes despite his smile.

The newspaper article that had been stored with the photo was dated November 8, 1988, twenty-four years ago. The story was about a gang fight in Kenwood, a neighborhood in the southeast side of Chicago and along the lake shore. The police had been able to break it up, but not soon enough to prevent nine casualties, luckily none of them innocent residents from the neighborhood. That didn't make sense, though. I distinctly remembered Marietta saying her brother had only been a passerby when he was shot, assuming that this was talking about the same gunfight he had gotten caught in. Maybe the reporter had been mistaken or the Foster family had paid off the newspapers to keep Derek out of it. Mr. Foster had always loved his privacy, after all. Maybe he had been on the side of the police and she just hadn't mentioned that part to me...hopefully. I didn't want to think he had been on the side of the gang.

A slight chill went up my spine. I really needed to find a way to get the photograph back to Marietta. Maybe it would give her some consolation with all of this dark stuff going on. It was a bit late to text Mark now. I made a mental note to tell him tomorrow that I wanted to give it to them.

I put the article and the photograph on my bookshelf so I wouldn't forget them. The shoot-out had happened about the same time Marietta had said Derek was shot by crossfire – in November, twenty-four years ago. It couldn't be coincidence that the article was placed in the back of the frame with the picture of the three of them. I'd be willing to bet someone had put it there in Derek's memory.

I locked Jesse away in his crate, giving him his water bowl and an extra pillow. He looked up at me, confused, before curling up on the soft cushions with a rawhide bone. I left the TV on at low volume and left to go climb into bed. I sighed and rolled over to go to sleep. Mr. Foster had been a good friend, at least to me. Even if other people didn't think he was a respectable man, that was the way I wanted to remember him.

Chapter 9

It was the scratching that woke me up. What started out as a light, almost imperceptible scrape grew louder until it was like someone was clawing the inside of my head. I rubbed my eyes and sat up, trying to focus through my groggy thoughts. The noises were coming from the living room. Jesse must be clawing at the door to his crate trying to get out. After a few nights of sleeping with me, he was already too used to it to tolerate being put back in the crate at night.

It might make him feel better if I went out to say 'hello.' I turned and slid my feet off of the side of the bed. When I stood, my nightshirt fell into place. It was too hot at night for pajama bottoms, even short shorts. As a kid, I had fallen asleep on summer nights in a big shirt and I guess it carried over to adulthood. I padded over to my bedroom door and opened it, heading out into the shadowy hallway between the living room and the kitchen.

I paused at the sight that met my eyes when I looked into the living room, which was dimly lit by the TV's glow. The couches looked like big, black masses. I could vaguely see Jesse's crate in the corner. I was expecting to see Jesse clawing at the door, but instead he was scrunched up in the corner. I padded forward a few steps, blinking away my blurry vision, and realized something else was there, close to the ground in front of the crate. It looked like a person crouched down over the crate. He was using a file on the thin bars directly over Jesse's head. That must have been the scratching noise that woke me up!

A low, rumbling sound could be heard underneath the scratching and I realized that Jesse was snarling, with an occasional low bark. Jesse had only growled once before in all the time I had known him - when he had growled at me in the corner after I walked Spotty. Bark at a passing truck, yes. But he had always seemed too good-natured for any aggressive behavior. The entire situation was so bizarre that I couldn't be sure if I was just dreaming.

That was the snarl of an angry dog, one who was determined to protect its territory. Jesse wasn't cowering. He was braced against the back of the crate, facing down the intruder. His lips were curled away from two rows of very sharp and very pointed teeth in a powerful jaw. I would never go within five feet of a dog that was looking at me like that. And this stranger was staring Jesse right in the face.

My sluggish mind finally caught up with me. This person had broken into my apartment. What the hell was I still doing, standing there in plain sight and wearing nothing but a t-shirt? The intruder was so caught up in whatever he was doing to the crate that they hadn't noticed me. I crept back towards the bedroom and slid the door closed, but not completely shut, afraid that the click would give me away. I could probably hide in the closet until they were gone. My heart was beating fast and my hands fumbled with my cell phone.

Who was I going to call? My fingers froze over the keypad. Maybe I was in shock, I couldn't think straight. My call log was the first thing that appeared on the screen. If I called 911, the intruder might hear me speaking and come in after me. I put my phone on silent and pressed the messaging button over Jennifer's name, hoping that she would be responsive enough at this ungodly hour to help me.

Are you awake? I wrote.

It was a couple moments before she answered. *Did that sound wake you up too? Do we have rats now or something?*

It's coming from my apartment. Someone's in here. I need you to call 911, I replied.

What do you mean? Someone broke into your place? she wrote.

I just need you to call 911. They'll hear me if I do it.

Do I need to come in there?

My fingers were shaking slightly as they flew over the keys. *No! Stay in your apartment and lock your door.*

Okay. Be careful. They might hurt you.

She was right. I knew she was right. But just thinking about abandoning Jesse made me sick. Yeah, I had only had the dog for a week, but my protective instincts were kicking in. If this person did something to hurt my new dog, I would never forgive myself. If I waited here for the police, they might arrive way too late. I knew it was irrational, but the only thing I could think of doing was getting out of here with Jesse!

My cell phone went dark as we disconnected. I dug through my backpack in the corner of the room for my mace. The company had given me a can just in case of an emergency against any person or any aggressive dogs. My mother and I had joked about buying a stun gun when I had first moved to the city. Now I really wished I had.

I slid the phone into my sleeping bra before heading back out into the living room. Just as I reached the entrance, the sound of the file stopped. The figure reached in through the new hole at the top of Jesse's crate. In his outstretched hand was the outline of a Milk Bone. He was trying to bait Jesse to come closer, but Jesse was having none of it.

I picked my way over behind the figure, praying that the floorboards wouldn't creak. With my eyes fixed on the dark shape, I didn't notice the plastic ball on the ground before I had unwittingly kicked it across the wooden floor. The bumps across the floorboards seemed louder than they should have been. It startled the stranger, who jerked his arm out and faced me, his outline looming a foot over me. I gasped, but a scream caught in my throat before it could force its way out. This would have been the perfect opportunity to use the mace, but I couldn't make the hand holding the can obey me and activate the switch.

He came towards me, not saying a word. He had to make his way around the sofa first and that gave me enough precious seconds to will my body into action. I put the couch between us, but I hadn't anticipated the figure to reach over and make a grab for me with a pair of long, ape-like arms. I felt strong fingers curl around my forearm, but luckily, it wasn't the arm with the mace. The touch sent a wave of panic through me and I screamed, which caused Jesse to start barking. If I'd been worried about the neighbors hearing me before, now I hoped they would! I felt the stranger's hand tense up and raised the mace at the same time he raised his free fist. I aimed the nozzle at his face and pressed on it. There was a hiss as the can released its contents followed by a pained grunt. A knife clattered to the floor.

He had been holding a knife. He could have *killed me* with that knife. My body wanted to freeze up again at the thought of how close I had come to being filleted, but the stranger shoved me backwards as he covered his face with his hands. Now was my chance. I threw myself at him and somehow managed to topple him over. I made for Jesse's crate. He was scrabbling at the door, trying to fix his jaw around the bars as though he could break out.

I almost expected Jesse to snap at me when I opened the door, but he let me loop my fingers through his collar. He resisted me for a second, not wanting to budge from where he was poised to attack the figure, but after a harder tug, he relented and followed me towards the front door. I jerked it open and dragged Jesse out, leaving the door wide open. The intruder fumbled his way toward me before I slammed it shut and shot down the stairs with Jesse in tow.

I led him to the front of the building, only coming to rest when we were on the sidewalk outside. The streetlight above us flickered as I glanced around, panting. Even at this late hour, there were a handful of cars on the road. I didn't care if I was wearing nothing but an oversized t-shirt. People would be able to see me if the intruder decided to chase me out here. True, I didn't know if they would actually try to help me if I needed it, but I didn't care. I stood in the middle of the walkway with my arms around Jesse until the police arrived.

A marked car pulled up to the curb five minutes later and two uniformed officers got out. I told them what had happened and they came with me upstairs to investigate. I held onto Jesse's collar all the while. He had calmed down, but he was shaking almost imperceptibly. The door to my apartment had been left gaping. I distinctly remembered slamming the door behind me. The intruder must have opened it, meaning he was probably gone by now.

They told me to wait in the hall while they searched around inside. I heard them open my closets and check around each room. The lock on my back door, which led to the rear stairwell, had been picked. If the intruder had tried to force it open, I probably would have awakened a lot sooner. If the lock had failed, the windows on either side of the door were large enough for a person to climb through, but I always kept them locked since they were right above the porch.

When the officers said the place was clear, I grabbed some pants and yanked them on. I didn't really want to stand around half-dressed while the officers took details for their report. At first glance, it didn't look like anything had been stolen. Jesse's crate was the only thing that had been disturbed. I did a quick check of my jewelry box and money stash. My computer was still there and my television hadn't been touched. I would have done a more thorough search, but I was still dead-tired. It seemed that all the intruder had been after was Jesse. I had no idea why, but it still pissed me off. What kind of person messed with someone's dog?

If he had wanted to take Jesse, he could have tried picking up the crate and carrying it. Although, the crate would probably have been too awkward to maneuver by himself in the middle of the night without making a ton of noise. Even then, he could have just opened the latch and dragged Jesse out. Instead, he had opted to saw his way into the crate for whatever reason. None of this made sense!

Once the police had all the information they needed from me, they went over to take a quick statement from Jennifer. Afterward, she came over to my place and we crashed in the living room. I was feeling too edgy to be alone in the apartment with just Jesse for the night. We checked twice to ensure that every door and window in both of our apartments was locked up tight.

Before settling in to try and sleep, I called Cheryl to tell her what had happened (even in the middle of the night, her line was open for emergencies). She was terribly concerned and asked me if I wanted her to find someone else to fill-in for my appointments the next day. She would probably take care of the early morning cat visit herself. I stopped to think about that for a long moment. I was fine, but after having my apartment broken into and somebody making an attempt on my life, I just wanted to sleep. I would need time to recuperate and make sure nothing else in the apartment had been screwed up, so I agreed.

As Jennifer left to get ready for work the next morning, I thanked her for staying with me and promised to get her a picture with the *Grimoire Danya* boys in return for her support. I got dressed and took Jesse for a walk. The sun was shining and the streets seemed obnoxiously cheerful after such an action-packed night. Why was it so hard just for my life to go back to normal, like it was before the murder?

Jesse stopped at his usual spot next to the front gate to go to the bathroom. I peered around at the grass to give him an ounce of privacy while he lifted his leg and saw something glint by the edge of the sidewalk. I knelt down to take a closer look and found an irritatingly familiar silver cylinder. Where it was laying was pretty close to the spot where Jesse and I had sat waiting for the police the night before. Sure enough, the one on Jesse's collar was gone. It must have fallen off in all the confusion. I put it back on his collar and we finished up outside.

I spent the rest of the day cleaning and searching through my belongings to see if there was anything out of place or missing, but everything from the fridge to my rattiest pair of socks was accounted for. It would have been funny if it wasn't so bizarre and the incident hadn't been so frightening. If I told my mother about this, she would probably insist that I get an alarm system like the one Mr. Foster had set up (even if said system hadn't been able to keep him alive in the end).

I called up my parents to let them know the latest happenings. My mother was freaked out, of course, and lamented the fact that I didn't have a muscular boyfriend to protect me. I reminded her that I had mace for self-defense. Still, buying a stun gun suddenly became less of a joke between us and more like a really good idea.

My mother insisted that I go to the hospital, but I assured her that I hadn't been harmed. Before, they had been fine with waiting until the end of the month to come and visit me, but now, things were getting too personal. I only just managed to assure them that an overnight trip was unnecessary after fifteen minutes of negotiation. We pushed the date to Friday, and only then with the promise that I would call them nightly to let them know I was alright.

I had plenty of time to finish unpacking the box of

dog supplies from Mark. The bottom was layered with treats, a small pack (I guessed for carrying poop bags), and a set of spare feeding bowls.

I dug around inside the satchel and, to my great surprise, found a pair of silver cylinders, the exact same size and shape as the one already on Jesse's collar. This was getting ridiculous! I was seeing these things everywhere now and I hadn't even heard of them until a few days ago! Why did James need three for Jesse, anyway? One would do the job of identifying Jesse well enough!

They opened up just like Jesse's and Spot's, but they were far from empty. Something had been rolled up and tucked inside both cylinders. I tipped them out to find two tight rolls of one-hundred dollar bills.

I had to stare at them and feel them in my hands just to make sure my imagination wasn't playing tricks on me. Was I still in shock from the break-in? I unrolled one of the bills and held it up to the light. The ghost image off to the side confirmed that they weren't fake. Who would stuff a bunch of money into such tiny containers? Was it for emergencies? Maybe this was some kind of screwed-up karma. I had been dragged through the wringer for the last week and now I was getting rewarded for surviving.

As eager as I was to take a bunch of twenties and ride off into the sunset, these cylinders had come directly from the home of a recently murdered man. I couldn't write this off as coincidence. Detectives Neal and Carl had given me numbers to contact them the first time we talked.

Once I told them about the break-in and about the strange money, they asked if they could come to my place and take a closer look. I was going to be there all day, so I told them it was all right. They were as polite as ever, fortunately. I wasn't sure how much I was allowed to ask about the investigation, so I just let them see the cylinders and the rolls of money first. When they asked me if I had found anything else strange in the box, I said no.

"Good thing you brought these to our attention, Ms. Gladdis," Carl said. "I believe we found what your robber was really after."

I tilted my head curiously. "You mean the money in the silver things?"

"Exactly," Carl said. "Was your dog wearing one of them last night?"

"Yeah, the one he's wearing right now. It fell off when we went outside in the middle of the night, but I found it while we were out this morning," I said. I retrieved the cylinder from Jesse so they could see it was empty.

"It fell off while you were waiting for the police? So, the intruder saw it but never had the chance to get a hold of it or look inside?" Neal said.

"I don't think so," I said.

Carl sighed and tucked the money back into their respective containers. "He wanted it because he probably recognized what it was. Do you know anything about these containers?"

I shrugged. "I've seen them around, but I thought they were for keeping ID chips in."

"That's what the dog owners will say, yeah," Neal said. "But they were all built to transport money, not tags."

"So, is it for banking or something?" I said, feeling a bit stupid for doing so, but I was getting the strong feeling there was something I was missing.

"In short, these cylinders," Neal said, holding one out in his palm, "Are used to trade drugs. It's a part of a dealing ring the police have been trying to bust recently."

I had to sit down at the dining room table so I could take a second to process that. Drugs were the last thing I had been expecting. "How does that work? I mean, wouldn't people start to realize this was going on if they saw everyone trading the containers?"

"Did you know what they were used for, before we told you? To an average person, it looks like a charm for a dog's collar or an ID tag, like you were told," Carl said.

"So how are the drugs exchanged? Do they pass around bags or what?" I asked.

"The key is to keep as low a profile as possible. If they make it obvious, it would be too easy for the police to spot when a deal was taking place. The containers are switched from the collar of the buyer's dog to the one on the seller's dog," Neal said. "It's supposed to make it subtle. The interaction can take place in a matter of seconds and out in the open. So, we suspect that is how the money changes hands, but as of yet, no one's been able to determine how the drugs are passed from the dealer to the buyer. Without that evidence, no one can be accused."

I nodded. Everything was coming together, though the implications were taking a while to sink in.

"I've seen it happen," I said, suddenly, thinking back to the dog park. I had seen a man swapping a cylinder from the collar of the German shepherd to the Dalmation. Had he really been in on some kind of drug deal? I hadn't been watching long enough to see if anyone had given him a bag or a container that might be holding drugs. I told the detectives about what I'd seen and the location of the dog park and they said it would be placed on a list of suspicious areas for the patrol to watch.

That left one more heavy question on my mind. "Does this mean that James Foster was in on the trade too? The cylinders came from his apartment, after all."

Carl nodded. "He was a person of interest in our VICE department for a while before his death. No solid evidence was found against him before now."

"Did he have any drugs in his apartment? I never thought he acted like he was using any," I said, though I only had a vague idea of the symptoms a drug abuser would have. I'd never thought he had pale skin or dark circles under his eyes. He seemed healthy for his age.

"Nothing was found during the initial investigation and another one held after all of James Foster's belongings had been removed," Neal said. "There's not a whole lot else we can go on. We have the money, but without the drugs, all we can say is that Mr. Foster had a strange way of storing his cash."

It was hard for me to imagine Mr. Foster having anything to do with a drug ring. But I had to admit, in the context of his life, it made a weird sort of sense. He was a reserved, wealthy man in the middle of a bustling city, one who was paranoid enough to have a security system protecting his apartment at all times. It was more than a little suspicious. I wanted to defend him or deny that he would have any part in a drug deal, but how much did I really know about him? I had heard of people wearing a different face at work as opposed to the one they wore at home. For all I knew, Mr. Foster could have been acting nice to me the entire time, just so I wouldn't suspect anything was wrong. Acting seemed to run in his family.

"I know another family who keeps a cylinder like this on their dog," I said. I told them about finding another cylinder on Spotty's collar and opening it to find a white powder inside.

"Thank you for your information," Carl said. "It's interesting that the cylinders would have any residue inside. They aren't normally used to carry the product because they're too small. It wouldn't be worth it."

Neal rubbed his jaw thoughtfully. "Unless the person who rolled up the money had some product on their hands. It got on the money and rubbed off on the container," he said. "They could have handled it beforehand and left such a small amount on their hands it went unnoticed."

"We'll look into it," Carl said. "Is there anything else you might be able to tell us, Ms. Gladdis?"

Between the realization that Mr. Foster might actually be a criminal and the feeling that I had betrayed Spotty's family, I was having a hard time thinking. My brain was jumbled with conflicting emotions. Was that why someone had tried to break into my apartment? They had been after the cylinder, thinking it might still have some money inside? It would explain why they had tried to make a hole in Jesse's crate to reach in rather than to just pull Jesse out. I told the detectives as much and they agreed that it was a plausible theory. Hard to believe such a small trinket could be the cause of so much chaos.

"If you happen to think of anything else, even if it seems small, call us. Don't try to investigate this by yourself," Carl said. "Dealers can look like normal people on the surface, but if you get too close, they feel threatened. They might think you suspect something, maybe that you even work for the police. You *have* been talking to us a lot lately, after all."

The robber from the previous night must have been after the cylinder because he thought it had money inside. But how had he known that Jesse was living with me and that I had the cylinders? Was he going to break in again? Should I go somewhere else for a while? Maybe now that he knew the police had come over, he would be scared off.

"What about the dogs? Being so close to the drugs can't be good for them, can it? Don't the owners care about them enough not to risk them getting sick?" I said.

"That doesn't stop anyone," Neal said, grimly.

For some reason, my thoughts turned back to my walk with Spot. When I had opened his cylinder, a little bit of the powder had found its way onto my hands and I had wiped them on my clothes. I couldn't help but remember how weird Jesse had acted that night, but maybe the problem with his behavior hadn't been due to him adjusting to a new home, but the scent of the powder.

"Do you know if dogs ever act aggressively if they smell or inhale the drugs?" I said.

"We haven't had a chance to study the effect on them, but it could be. They might not get the same high as humans, but they might get very sick if they are exposed to enough," Carl said.

That didn't explain Jesse's weird aggression, though. If whomever had broken into my apartment had been part of the drug ring, then there was a chance they had the scent of the drugs, if not the drugs themselves, on their clothes. What if the problem he had wasn't with the drugs, but with the emotions he associated with the drugs? It was common for dogs to act defensively around something they associated with pain or fear, like yelling or objects used to hurt them. If triggered, they might snap and attack.

Mr. Foster might have been kind to Jesse, but what about his "colleagues," the people he dealt with if he was trading drugs? Would someone big and intimidating have been as nice to a dog? Any number of them could have been enraged over a deal and done something to harm

Jesse, which would make him associate the drugs with negativity.

Enough for him to act grumpy when he smelled them on me, I thought. I explained all of this to the detectives and they agreed it was plausible.

Neal looked as though he was turning an idea over in his mind. "If that's true, then we might be able to utilize it."

I looked at him, bewildered. "How? I mean, I guess Jesse could be a police dog and sniff people out, but I think that might scare him more."

"Not like that," Neal replied. "But if there's any chance at all that James Foster had a cache of product in his apartment that we weren't able to find, your dog might be able to help us find it."

I hadn't thought of that before. It seemed safe enough, especially if the detectives would be there with us during the search. "The police thought they were just investigating a murder, but when Mr. Foster's name came up, did they think that would be a good time to look for the drugs? If the drugs didn't turn up during the initial investigation, where else could they be?"

"It still might be worth a shot to do another search now that everything's been moved out," Neal said. "If you'd grant us permission to use your dog in this investigation, we would be grateful. You would be invited to come as well, to control the dog and to watch for any signs of the aggression you describe."

To be part of an actual police investigation...it was a thrilling thought, even if we weren't heading into the heart of danger. I readily agreed. If there was any way I could help them, I would. I wanted to see this mystery through to the end.

Chapter 10

The detectives had me follow along behind them to Evanston with Jesse in my car. When we arrived at the apartment building, I was struck by how little the place had changed, considering everything that had happened. The bushes lining the building looked neatly trimmed and the cars in the parking lot were clean and polished. It was like I was just coming back from a walk and was now about to take Jesse back up to Mr. Foster. What if we found something that would prove without a shadow of a doubt that Mr. Foster had actually been a part of a drug ring? It was almost too much to consider, but it was too late to back out now.

The detectives spoke with Elle Jones, whom I remembered from the outset of all this as the building manager. She had apparently been keeping the apartment clean until she could find another tenant. The cleaners had finished their work by now, which made my heart sink.

What if they had washed away any scent trail Jesse could have picked up? She said they had mostly been focused on getting the bloodstains out of the bedroom. They hadn't had to do much cleaning in the other rooms other than washing out the wine stains in the hall. Maybe we still had a chance after all.

The alien feeling of familiarity from outside became ten times worse when we got up to the apartment. From habit, my first inclination was to go over to the control panel on the wall and shut off the alarm, but the sound of beeping never came. They must have shut it off so the detectives could come and go as they pleased. The couches and chairs were gone. The walls had been stripped; the TV had been taken from its mount on the wall.

Jesse sniffed at the air and the carpet. With me holding the leash, he went around to the kitchen and the bedroom. I wondered how well he could remember his old home without the furniture or his things. Did he expect his old master to be here? We made a loop around the bedroom and came back, the detectives were never far behind. Every time Jesse paused to sniff at a certain spot, the detectives would comb through the area thoroughly. Jesse led me back to the living room and then paused to look out of the windows. It took a moment of petting and encouragement to get him back on track.

He kept sniffing around the spots where the couch and his food bowls had been. While we were wandering near the corner, Jesse started picking at the carpet with his claws. I went to stop him, but it looked as though this may not have been the first time he had done that. There was a section of the plush carpet, about a foot in diameter, that had been frayed and torn. As I remembered, there had been a soft, cushioned chair sitting over this very spot before. My parents would try moving furniture over our cat's favorite peeing spot to try to prevent accidents. Maybe Mr. Foster had been trying to keep Jesse from scratching the carpet by moving the chair over it.

Something else was off, though. As I watched Jesse run his paws over the carpet, I noticed the edge along the wall lifted slightly. The sealant had come off the carpet and the lining separated from the floor. I brought it to the attention of the detectives and they worked together to rip the carpet back. Built into the floor was a metal container, about the same size and shape of a shoebox. It was locked tight and the crease around the lid led to a keypad in the top.

"We've found his stash," Neal said, smirking in victory.

Carl experimented with the buttons for a moment. It looked like the safe had a five-letter word lock. I used a lock like this one to keep my bike tires secured to the frame to discourage anyone from stealing them, but that lock had a spinner-combination whereas this keypad was electronic.

"Any ideas?" Carl said.

"Probably something he would remember, something close to him," Neal said.

We tried the obvious stuff: Mr. Foster's first name;

the name of his son, Derek; and the name of his birth month…nothing worked. We spent a good twenty minutes trying whatever words came to mind before I had a sudden hunch. After all, who was the one that Marietta said had been the most important to James; the "star of his life", she had said. *Jesse.* Jesse's name wasn't the traditional spelling of "Jessie," either – I remembered seeing it spelled "Jesse" on James's profile in Best Furry Friends's database. If Jesse had been spelled the traditional way, it would have had six letters instead of five, so it wouldn't fit the keypad combination.

    I leaned forward and quickly typed in the five letters J-E-S-S-E. There was a click and the crease popped open. Neal opened it up the rest of the way to reveal several plastic bags containing white powder and a stringy leaf-like substance. I gasped and held Jesse back from sniffing the bags. He started growling as he retreated to the other end of the room with his tail tucked between his legs. Whatever he had been through had left a mark, that much was plain enough and it broke my heart. What kind of monsters hurt a dog over a bunch of plants?

    "Jackpot," Neal said. The detectives took pictures of the safe before putting on two pairs of rubber gloves to collect the bags as evidence.

    "His family…are they in on this too?" I said, my voice trembling slightly.

    "The Foster family has been under investigation for possible ties into the drug ring for years, but they cover their tracks very well," Carl said.

"Why didn't they pick up his stash while they were here?" I said. That would have been my first act, if I was in their place. The family had been clearing out Mr. Foster's apartment, just as Mark had said. They would have ample time to search for the box, unless they just hadn't been aware of the safe's existence at all. Mr. Foster had been hiding the cache for his own protection. Though that sparked the question: who would he need protection from? His family? Rival drug dealers? It was too difficult to say, now.

"Now that, I don't know, but you have to admit, it works out better for us," Carl said. "We have to go back to the precinct to have this processed. You're free to go if you want. Thank you for your cooperation, Ms. Gladdis."

I shook their hands, feeling a sense of... accomplishment. Pride that I had actually done something to help the police. But underneath that was dread as I forced myself to accept the truth. James Foster was a criminal, a drug dealer. That smiling face that I had seen almost every day for the last five months had been harboring this secret. He had been meeting with all sorts of characters, some very unsavory, and trading with them for who knew how long.

I couldn't help but wonder if the rest of his family had known about any of this. What if they had even been involved somehow? What if the reason Derek Foster had been killed in that shoot-out was because he had been part of the fight instead of a civilian unlucky enough to get caught in the crossfire? Marietta probably knew the truth if she had been a part of the 'family business.' Was it still going on now? Was Marietta trading drugs like her father? And if she was, did that mean that Rick and Mark were involved as well?

Everything I knew was unraveling at the seams. How was I supposed to feel about all of this, especially when it came to the boys? For so long, I had been gushing over their looks, their wit, the originality over their work... They had both seemed like honest people, but then again, so had Mr. Foster. What if Rick and Mark had shared his secret? Was that the reason they had such a big budget? They sold drugs?

My father and I had had a conversation once, when I was first thinking of moving to the city. His words came drifting lazily, condescendingly, to the front of my mind. *"You know how they get the money for all this? Selling drugs."* He had been talking about luxury condos at the time, but he may as well have been talking about *Grimoire Danya*.

I almost didn't have the heart to tell Jennifer about what we found. Luckily, I had the afternoon and evening to figure out what I was going to tell her. Jesse slept on the couch beside me, his head propped up on my leg. When my cell phone buzzed and played its text-message jingle, I jumped. Speak of the devil, it was from Jennifer.

Rick just tweeted. We're gonna get a new episode tonight! EEEEEE!

There was a time when a message like that would have had me rolling around on the floor and squealing like a little girl who had been gifted a puppy. Now, there was a lead weight crushing my heart. For the first time in the past three years, I didn't want to watch the update. I had fallen in love with the series and now I couldn't think about it without feeling sick.

I messaged Jennifer back and told her that I couldn't wait. I fixed dinner for Jesse and myself mechanically and wasn't surprised when it tasted like cardboard in my mouth. *Grimoire Danya* always updated every other week on Monday at 7 o' clock. With that schedule, Jennifer was right, tonight was the night for a new entry. When seven rolled around, I waited for my phone to ping me with a notification that a video had been uploaded. Ten minutes later, there was still nothing. After another twenty minutes, I asked Jennifer if she knew what was going on. She had no idea. From the looks of the online forums, the fandom was freaking out.

Eight o' clock rolled around without any word. After two hours of waiting, my mind was already creating images of either Mark or Rick laying on the floor of their warehouse unconscious from a drug overdose. Maybe the detectives had come and picked them up for serious questioning. I had to know or I risked driving myself insane!

Staring at my phone, I realized that I could ask Mark if there was something wrong. Could I do it, though, knowing what I knew? What if he figured out I was onto him? Maybe it would look more suspicious if I didn't ask at all. Better to make it look as though everything was normal. Gathering up my courage, I sent him a text: Hey there! I hope I'm not bothering you, but I noticed you guys sent a tweet out about an update tonight and nothing's been posted. Is everything all right?

    The knot of tension in my gut tightened a little when I forced myself to hit the green 'send' button. It was out of my hands, now. Either Mark was going to tell me the truth or he wasn't. I was just another fan to him, after all. I just happened to be the fan who walked his grandfather's dog and then found said grandfather dead in his bedroom. Not exactly an ideal basis for a friendship.

    Whatever was happening seemed to be taking up all of Mark's attention (which didn't make me feel any better). He didn't get back to me until I had already gotten ready for bed and was curled up beside Jesse. My phone rang and I answered it, giving a tired "hello." I hadn't checked the caller ID, so when Mark's voice responded, it surprised me and I sobered instantly.

    "Hey there. Sorry, did I wake you up? I just need to talk to someone right now and I didn't know who else to call," Mark said. His voice sounded strained.

    "No! It's okay," I insisted. Despite everything that had happened that day, my heart still fluttered at the sound of him saying those words. It was slightly flattering that he had thought to respond to my text message at all. "Did something happen?"

    "Our uncle was arrested for killing our grandfather tonight," he said. No beating around the bush with this one, we were getting straight to the point.

    "Your uncle?" I repeated, dumbly. "You mean Jim?"

"Yeah, Uncle Jim. They're saying he killed him over a financial disagreement, but we all know the truth," Mark said, bitterly.

I hesitated before saying, slowly, "What's the truth?"

It was a long moment before he replied. "Look, I don't know how much you know about our family, but there's a damn good reason we've tried to cut ourselves off from grandpa and our uncle."

"I understand, you don't have to tell me if you don't want to," I said, trying to sound soothing.

"My mother tried so hard to get away from them while she was pregnant with Rick. She told me they threatened her that if she didn't stay quiet, they would kill her. She was scared, so she tried to leave," Mark said.

I swallowed nervously, "Mark? Who threatened your mother?"

"Grandpa did, and Uncle Jim. It's like mother said, Jim was the one most loyal to grandpa. He was pretty much grandpa's errand boy, from the sounds of it," Mark said, disdainfully.

"But if your uncle was so loyal, why would he kill Mr. Foster?" I asked.

"I don't know. It doesn't make sense but the police don't care about the motive right now," Mark said. "They found a knife in a gun store that our uncle runs. They were questioning him about some…activity that was going on last night. While they were there, they saw some knives that were the same size and shape as the one that was used to stab grandpa. One was missing. They had a warrant for his store because of another investigation, so they searched the place and found the murder weapon in Jim's office. Someone had tried to clean the blade but there was a little bit of blood on the guard and it had Jim's fingerprints."

I could tell where this was going. "Did they test the blood? Was it Mr. Foster's?

"Yeah, it was," Mark said, with a sigh.

I had no idea what to say, but eventually managed to say, "Well, it sounds like they caught the killer. That should be a relief."

"It should, but mother's having a really rough time," Mark said.

I was a little confused at that. If Mr. Foster and Jim had once threatened her, I should think that Marietta would be relieved that they were both out of her way. But I didn't want to tell that to Mark and sound insensitive.

"I'm sorry for her," I said, sincerely. "How is Rick doing?"

"Rick was brought in for questioning tonight. That's the reason we didn't get the newest entry uploaded," he said.

"He was arrested too? Why?!" I said.

"No, not arrested. They just wanted to ask him about our uncle. The police think that our Jim may have tried to steal a prop knife out of our warehouse to frame Rick for the murder," Mark said.

"Seriously? That's horrible! What kind of uncle is he?"

"The kind that threatens his sister and doesn't talk to us for years and years," Mark said, flatly. "I don't care why he did it. Him and his men…that entire side of the family, really, has always been bad news. It was only a matter of time before they tried to drag my mother back into their problems."

"What was he going to say to frame Rick? The police wouldn't believe that!" I said, stunned. "They'd have to come up with a pretty good excuse as to why Rick would kill him."

"Grandfather sent us a little money to help with the web series but didn't care about us beyond that. They could say Rick killed him out of spite. Not that it really matters anymore," he said.

"I see…" I said, unsure of what to say. "What about you? How are you doing?"

"I've been better," Mark said. "It's just…once word gets out about this, we can kiss *Grimoire Danya* goodbye. Rick's been working his butt off for the series. He quit the job he had before so he could work on it full-time. We had plenty of money coming in to support ourselves. It wasn't that he was worried about…"

"…Worried about what? Money?" I said.

Mark sighed. "Someone finding out where we

came from. What our family does. You know about it already, don't you?"

I nibbled on my lip. Had Mark seen through me? "What makes you say that?"

"I can tell. There's no reason you wouldn't know by now. You work with all those dogs. You've seen the money containers, right?" he asked.

He must have been tired enough to start firing shots in the dark. What if he was trying to find out how much I knew? He said he and Rick had pulled away from that lifestyle, but what if he was lying? If I refused to admit I knew the truth, it might be suspicious. I'd already been attacked in my own home once, I didn't want to go through that again.

"I'm sorry, it's getting really late. I should be getting to sleep," I said.

"Wait, April," he said. Maybe it was the slightly exasperated way he said my name, but I stayed on the phone. "I'm sorry. You don't have to tell me anything. It's just…be careful from now on. These people are all over the place and they won't feel guilty about silencing you if they think they have a good reason. You don't want to get involved with them."

Get involved with you, you mean? I thought.

"All right, I won't," I said. "But before we go, I need you to tell Marietta that I have something for her. A picture of her and her brothers fell into the box you gave to me."

"I can give you her number," Mark said. "Her house is all the way south in Chatham, but she's been staying up in Evanston while she figures out what to do with the rest of grandpa's things. It would be easier for you to meet her there."

I thanked him, took down Marietta's number, and promptly flopped onto my pillows after we hung up. I was drained, physically and mentally. How could the detectives deal with things like this every day?

I sent a message to Jennifer to let her know that Rick and Mark were dealing with legal trouble that had to do with the murder and promised to fill her in later. I would call up Marietta in the morning and see if I could meet with her within the next few days before she went home to Chatham. It would be a long drive for me if I waited too long. I could mail the photograph and the newspaper article, yeah, but there were things I wanted to ask her that could only be asked face-to-face.

Chapter 11

Marietta would be in Evanston for another two days. Over the phone, she sounded just as exhausted as Mark, though I couldn't tell if that was from stress or if it was just her usual, sleepy tone. I called her during my lunch break the day after my conversation with Mark. She agreed to meet me in a park near the hotel she was staying in. It was beautiful and public, which made me feel safer. The idea of meeting with her made me nervous, but I was desperate for answers. Maybe it was my love for *Grimoire Danya* that was driving me forward; the hope that I could prove she and her sons weren't evil and wanted by the law.

My pet sitting visits that day lasted until the early afternoon. It was a relief seeing all of the puppies and dogs I had come to know and love. It was comforting to know that they were happy and cared-for while everything else in this city was chaotic. Looking at the sweet face of a little Yorkie puppy that fit in the palm of my hand, it was easy to forget about any drugs and murders.

It wouldn't be long before the police questioned Spot's parents about the cylinders, if they followed the tip I gave them. Cheryl would probably be notified about the fact that one of our clients had been taken into custody. She was smart; maybe she would figure out that this had something to do with me and want to talk about it. I wasn't sure if I was looking forward to that conversation or dreading it.

The time slot that had once been filled with Jesse's afternoon visits was now taken over by a chubby beagle with ears that hovered in the air like a plane when a strong wind picked them up. It provided me with much needed laughter. Once I had finished the walk and taken him home, I drove up to Evanston to meet with Marietta.

The park was small, but there were families with children playing in the grass and under the large oak trees. If I was worried about Marietta having back-up from a gang, I doubted they would disguise themselves as these run-of-the-mill people. No one had trench coats or guns like the old gangster movies. Then again, the people at the dog park had looked average, too, but they were apparently neck-deep in the drug trade.

I found Marietta standing by her car in the parking lot. She was wearing a light, summer dress with cheerful colors that brought out the color in her cheeks. Compared to her, I was sweaty and unappealing. Funny how the image of her in my mind always stuck her in the heavy, black dress she had worn at the funeral. She turned to me and smiled when I got out of the car. Honestly, I hadn't expected her to agree to meet with me, but maybe the photograph meant more to her than I thought.

"Hello, April. I'm glad to see you're doing well," Marietta said.

"Thanks. I heard about your brother. I'm sorry it turned out this way," I said. She nodded, her smile fading.

"It was inevitable," she said. "I should have known it was him when he didn't come to Father's funeral. Jim was his favorite out of all of us. Father left everything to him in his will. There was no reason he wouldn't come but for a guilty conscience. I don't feel sorry for him at all. He tried to blame Rick for his own actions, but both Rick and Mark were visiting me on the day of the murder. He couldn't have done it."

"I believe you. But do you think that was why Jim killed your father? To get what Mr. Foster left to him in his will?" I asked.

Marietta sighed deeply, her proud face softened by sadness. "He's not the same boy we knew when we were children. Not the same at all."

After a moment, I decided it was time to give her back the photograph and the newspaper article. They were handed over as two separate pieces rather than together in the same frame. The picture of Jesse had a new home on my windowsill. "I got a new frame for the photograph," I said. "The other one broke when Jesse and I were playing."

"It's all right. I'm glad to have them back," she

said.

"Did they belong to you first?" I asked.

"Yes. I sent them to my father. I wanted to remind him of us. He was worrying me...although I don't know why. He didn't deserve anyone worrying about him, really. But all I could think of was the man who loved me when I was a little girl. I wished we could mend things between us, even a little bit. But it was all in vain," she said.

"You left them after Derek died, right? I saw the article in there...was he involved in that gunfight?" I said. The question had been bothering me for days, but a sudden flash of fear made me wish I could take it back.

Marietta's eyes searched my face for a moment before she said, "Yes, he was. That's how father raised us, especially Jim; so we could take over his business. Jim became his right-hand man and Derek was his helper."

"What about you?" I said.

"I was only seventeen when Derek died. Not nearly old enough to know what I was doing. I couldn't think of any other way to live," she said. "At that time, I was five months pregnant with Rick. I was more scared for my unborn child than I was for myself. The father was...I don't remember his name. It was one of Jim's friends from overseas who just wanted a fling. I was foolish enough to give in to him. After I had Rick, I met my late husband. We married a year later and I had Mark. Without those boys, I would have given up long ago."

"I'm glad they've been able to help you for all these years. I feel the same way with my mom," I said.

She smiled at me. "Children should mean the world to their mothers. It's good that you feel the same way for yours."

I really wanted to try and comfort her, so I said, "When you say that you gave Mr. Foster – your father, I mean - that photograph to remind him of you, did it work? It was tucked into the back of another picture frame for safe-keeping. I think he liked it."

Marietta looked a little surprised. "Did he? I thought he would tear it up and throw it away. I hoped it would make him want to talk to me again. Maybe he wanted to fix things, after all. Change his way, you know? Maybe that's too much to hope for...but it's a nice thought."

Had he really changed his mind and never gotten the chance to act on it before he was murdered? The pieces were slowly coming together. For a man to be loyal to his father and then want to kill him would warrant a dramatic change. Jim had been raised as a criminal like Marietta and Derek, but unlike them, he had succeeded. But then, out of the blue, his father had started having second thoughts when faced with the memory of his first son. Had he blamed himself for Derek's death? I wondered if Marietta's gift had made him consider pulling out of the drug ring, realizing that it wasn't worth it in light of what he had already lost. Would it be enough to convince Jim to kill his father, knowing that he could lose everything in his father's will if his father disowned his criminal son?

As I was mulling this over, something else occurred to me.

"You know, I haven't been hearing about this case on the news. My mom follows the newspaper every day and she hasn't heard anything about it, either," I said.

"That would be our work. We like our privacy; you saw it with my father," Marietta said. "Even if the story was broadcast on the news, a little bit of money changing hands was enough to keep my father's name out of it."

"This is true. At least the press will leave you alone now," I said. I let the subject drop and was about to thank Marietta for her time and get back in my car when I caught a glimpse of another figure headed straight towards us. Somehow, Rick looked even more pale and sallow than when he had been covered with make-up as an injured Dyllas. He fixed me with a passive stare and nodded in greeting before looking at Marietta. "Did you get the picture?"

"Yes, dear. Come, let's go home. You look dreadful," Marietta said, gesturing towards the car.

"Is everything all right?" I asked, gripping my hands together to keep them from fidgeting.

Rick waved the concern aside. "I'm fine. Just coming down with something. At least we don't have to film again until this weekend. I can work out the bug."

"I hope you get better soon," I said. "I...I'm sorry about your uncle."

He blinked and then frowned at Marietta. "You didn't tell her about that, did you?"

"It doesn't matter, dear," she said.

"Yes, it does," Rick insisted. "We're keeping that stuff out of the news for a reason!"

Crap. I hadn't thought of the fact that I wasn't supposed to know about Jim when I first talked to Marietta! Did they know Mark had told me? I wasn't about to let that slip.

"I won't tell anyone, I promise," I said.

"There, see? Nothing to worry yourself over," Marietta said. "Now let's go. I'm feeling drained from this heat." She guided Rick back to the car with a hand on his arm.

"I'll see you later. Good luck with the series!" I said, to which Rick glanced over his shoulder with a nod of acknowledgment. They were out of the parking lot by the time I pulled away from the curb.

Chapter 12

In the public's eye, the case was closed with the arrest of Jim. It was over. I just wanted to go home and sleep for a week. Part of me was relieved that Rick, Mark, and their mother weren't actually criminals themselves. Jennifer was hounding me for answers, but I told her that I had a headache and just wanted to rest. I told her that the boys would probably update that night now that they had finished dealing with the police and asked if she would let me borrow the first season of *Grimoire Danya*. I was desperate for some nostalgia.

After Jesse's evening walk, we settled down on the couch while the DVD menu came up. I didn't bother with the extras, just played the show. I had wanted a return to the way things had been, right? The episodes were only ten minutes long during the first season. Everybody looked so young, even though the series had only started out three years ago. The production quality was good, but it was at a time before they had bought the expensive cameras and hired an official film crew.

Actually, the first few episodes didn't have Averad in them at all. Dyllas was the one who carried the show. It was weird, comparing the Rick I saw from back then to the way I knew him now. He must have been going through some strength training or something – there were a lot more stunts performed in the late seasons and Rick would have had to prepare for them. The Rick on the screen was thinner, his arms skinny, and his skin didn't have the bronzed tan that Dyllas had in recent updates.

I looked up a picture of him from the latest episode on my phone. He looked strong enough to climb those cliffs from the third season or swim in the icy lake in the fourth. For some reason, I thought back to the chain-link fences near the beach around Mr. Foster's apartment building. Someone built like Rick, with his stunt experience, would have no problem scaling the fence. All they would need is time…

Why was I thinking about this? It didn't mean anything. Just because Rick could do something like that didn't mean he would actually do it in real life. It certainly didn't mean he had murdered his grandfather. It had been his uncle, Jim, who had wanted to silence his father before he was blotted out of the will. Before everything they had worked for was lost.

But then I remembered Mark saying something like that too, about Rick. He had said that Rick was so obsessed over *Grimoire Danya*, doing everything in his power so it wouldn't fail. Just look how determined he was to keep this case out of the news. Just one mention of their family's involvement in the drug ring would signal the end for the entire series.

I shook my head. It was crazy to think this way. There was no way Rick could be the murderer...but I had to be sure. It was too late to call on Jennifer to run my ideas past her. I wound up texting Mark at a late hour again.

Hey there. Just making sure everything is okay.

If I wasn't careful, he might think this was going to be a common occurrence and the last thing I wanted was to scare him off if it was going to irritate him. But it was just a text! He didn't have to answer it until the morning if he didn't want to (if he responded at all). Besides, he had sounded so tired during our last call that I couldn't help but worry a little. If there was any way I could help alleviate his stress, I would do it in a heartbeat.

To my amazement, he called me, just as he had the night before. This time, his voice was hushed.

"April, listen to me. I don't have a whole lot of time to talk right now," he said.

"What? What's going on?" I said, uneasily.

"I'm nervous about Rick, he's been acting weird and tense all day," he said.

"About what?" I said. The case was closed, why would Rick be upset now?

"He says he's been getting some threatening

messages from people who say he set our uncle up. He wants to call the police to find them," Mark said.

"The police won't do anything about what people say on Facebook, will they?" I said. "And it's not true, so why is he so uptight?"

"Because…I don't know. I told him that's what he should do, to chill out, but he's not listening to me. You don't know him like I do. He's out of his mind!" he said.

"Okay, don't worry," I said. "What's he doing right now?"

"He left for the warehouse an hour ago," he said. "I haven't heard from him since. Listen…when he left, I think he had a knife with him."

"A knife? What on earth is he doing with a knife?" I said.

"Well, thing is, we lost one of our knives from our inventory a week ago," Mark said.

"Around the time your grandfather was found in his room?" I said, with a sinking feeling.

"Remember when I said the police had raided a weapons shop our uncle owned? They went there because they were tracking down the knife stolen from us," Mark said.

"What are you saying?" I asked, my voice trembling a bit.

"That day, Rick took a knife into that shop to get it polished and repaired," he said.

"You think it was the same one?" I asked.

"The police found the receipt for it at the weapons shop that Rick forgot. I think Rick chose that place because he was hoping to finagle a discount out of our uncle, but the knife never found its way back," Mark said.

This was all happening too fast. I had to take a deep breath to calm down. "Your mother said both of you were visiting her that day. How could he be at the gun shop?"

"I don't doubt that. But trust me, he wasn't with us. That was what our mother wanted us to tell everyone," Mark said.

"Why?"

"So Rick wouldn't have suspicion cast on him."

"Why are you telling me all of this?" I asked, now tense.

"April, I'm pretty sure you and I know things that would be able to turn this entire case around and he knows that we know," Mark said.

"He does? How would he know anything about me?"

"I don't know if you've realized this, April, but you've had someone following you for the last two months," Mark said.

I felt the blood drain from my face as I listened to him. Who on earth would take interest in a random dog walker?

"Think about it," Mark continued. "How else would the murderer have been able to know when you were coming to our grandfather's apartment? They plotted it all out *according to your arrival times*."

"How do you know this?" I asked.

"Because I've been watching Rick when he's around you and I've heard him talking to the detectives. I think Rick knows the truth and he's clamming up. He knows it wasn't our uncle who murdered grandfather," he said.

"Does he know who it really was, then?" I said, but his response was interrupted by my door bell ringing.

"Was that your doorbell? Don't answer that," Mark said.

"I'm not," I said, irritably. Did he think I was an idiot? "It's the middle of the night!"

"I'm coming over there. What's your address?" he said.

"Do you think it's him?"

"Either him or someone else who's been keeping their eye on you. Turn off all of your lights. Call the police if they keep wanting to get in," he said.

The buzzer rang again. I was getting scared now. "How long is it going to take you to get here?" I said. I had no intention of letting him up into my apartment, either. For all I knew, Mark was lying and he was the one knocking, waiting for me to let him up.

"It's midnight. Traffic is light. I should get there in twenty minutes," he said. "I'm serious. Don't let anyone in unless it's the police."

"I won't. I won't," I said, before I heard him hang up. With a pounding heart, I went around my apartment turning off all the lights. The buzzer and the sound of my frantic voice had finally woken Jesse from his sleep in the corner and, at the sound of the next ring, he leaped up and started barking. I winced at the sharp sound and pulled him into the bathroom.

For the next several minutes, there was nothing. I hoped whomever it was had gotten the hint and left. Fat chance, I knew. I tried to close the door on Jesse to keep him in the bathroom, but he stuck his muzzle out, preventing me from closing the door. The second I opened the door wider so his head wasn't crushed, he pushed past me and headed directly towards the kitchen, where he stood barking at the back door.

My phone buzzed in my hand and I nearly jumped out of my skin.

"April! What's going on over there?" Jennifer said.

"I…I think someone else is trying to break in," I said.

"What? Again?" she said.

"Yes, I think they're at my back door," I said.

"Well, get off the phone with me and call the police! If you don't do it, I will!" Jennifer said.

"Okay, okay! I'm doing it now!" I said. I hung up and dialed 911. About midway into my explanation, there was a bang on the door that made me gasp. I finished up the call, even with Jesse barking frantically and clawing the door. There was a loud curse and I heard the sound of heavy footsteps retreating down the staircase. I opened the blinds of a window and dared to look outside. There was no one on the porch now. I nudged Jesse behind me while I opened it up a tad to peer outside, enough to make absolutely sure the coast was clear.

From somewhere down below, I could hear angry voices drifting up to me, voices that I could recognize from anywhere.

"I can't believe this! What the hell are you doing here?" Mark said.

"I'm covering up loose ends! Didn't I tell you that's what I would do?" Rick said.

"You call her a loose end?"

"She knows everything now! She could go to the press! I know you've been talking to her!"

"Yeah, I was talking to her about our mother! Nothing else!" Mark said.

"Oh, really? Then what the hell are you doing here? She told you where she lived!"

"Because she heard you clomping around and she got scared. What were you going to do, anyway? Just waltz in and stab her?" Mark said. My throat closed at that.

When Rick didn't say anything, Mark continued. "You've been acting weird ever since you talked with Uncle Jim. What did he say to you?!"

"He told me enough and he was right! The old man was going to ruin everything for us! Everything you and I worked for would be gone right now! Do you want that?" Rick yelled.

"No, but I didn't want him to die, either! Did Jim tell you that the only way to fix all of this was to kill him? Oh god…it was you, wasn't it?" Mark said.

"Shut up, Mark."

"You killed him."

"You and Mom said you would cover for me no matter what happened!" Rick shouted.

"Only because I thought our uncle framed you! I didn't think you were actually capable of doing it! But look at you right now!" Mark said.

I sunk down on my knees on the floor, my hand covering my mouth. A rushing filled my ears. It was Rick. It was Rick. Rick killed Mr. Foster.

"Get away from here, Mark."

"No, this has gone far enough. I'm not like you! I can't keep doing this when I'm off camera. You have to turn yourself in!" Mark said.

"I'm not doing anything that isn't necessary! I'm trying to protect us, Mark! The old man didn't care about us anyway! No one's going to miss him," Rick said. "He was fine at first, sure, but then he got that dog, and suddenly we didn't matter! Look what she could have told the police!"

"And you think this is going to fix everything?!" Mark exclaimed. "If you kill her, that will be more evidence the police can use against you! Just get out of here!"

"Not until she's gone and that damn dog shuts up! Either she goes or I go!"

I heard Mark's voice lower to a lethal calm. "That can be arranged."

The sounds of a scuffle followed. I couldn't resist anymore. I flung open the back door and looked down over the railing of the staircase. Rick and Mark were in the alley and I could barely tell them apart in the dim light. I remembered that Mark had worked out for a long time too to get ready for his role, just as much as Rick. God, I hoped he was enough to be able to hold Rick back. I called out both of their names. One of the figures glared up at me. An alley lamp lit up his face and I could tell it was Rick. The knife he was holding had the same, modified design and color scheme as the other knives in the *Grimoire Danya* inventory. It was the missing knife.

Rick's moment of distraction gave Mark just the opportunity he needed to grab Rick's knife arm and wrenched it to the side. Rick cried out and dropped the knife to the ground with a clatter. It was just then that I heard police sirens coming closer and I rushed back into the apartment to join Jesse in the bathroom.

A bit later, I got a call from Mark saying that Rick had fled from the scene when he heard the sirens. Mark was injured, but he'd been able to slow Rick down and take the knife before he could get it back. I went out to wait with him until an ambulance came to take him to the hospital so his stab wound could be treated. Jennifer sat with me for the rest of the night while we waited for more news.

When the police heard the story of what happened that evening, the patrols went on a search for Rick. They finally found him in the *Grimoire Danya* studio, trying to gather some papers before running off. The following day, we found out that Rick had confessed to everything and told exactly how James Foster's death had played out.

It seemed that their Uncle Jim was a firm supporter of the drug-dealing ring that Mr. Foster had tried to pull away from. He thought Marietta had already convinced her father to reveal damning information to the authorities about the drug trade.

Jim wanted to get rid of any evidence his father might have in his apartment to make sure he couldn't go to the police. Jim knew about the existence of the safe and the money containers, but he didn't know exactly where they were located and didn't want to risk his father expecting this kind of dirty business from him.

Rick knew that Marietta tried to talk her father into quitting the business, but Rick didn't know his grandfather's reaction. Somehow, Jim got in contact with Rick and told him that if Mr. Foster went to the police, everything Rick, Mark, and Marietta had worked for would be blown out of the water. Everyone would know how closely their family was tied in with the drug trade. He said that if Rick wanted to avoid the negative publicity, Rick had to go along with the plan to sneak into the apartment and steal the evidence. Mr. Foster wouldn't give the drugs or the money to anyone, so this was the only way to secure their secrets. Jim thought that if James caught Rick, he wouldn't hurt him because Rick was his grandson and incapable of doing much damage, so James would let Rick go. If Jim went, on the other hand, and was caught, then the consequences would be more dire, in the form of the police being called, or a death match between the two of them.

Rick agreed to all of this and told no one of the plan. He was just going to get the evidence and then deliver it to Jim. After that, he could go back to his life and be assured that *Grimoire Danya* was in no danger.

Mr. Foster, however, began to suspect he might be a target and made a plan to get the drugs out of his apartment. For one, he put a wad of cash into a couple of Jesse's cylinders. He was going to give the cash to "trusted individuals" who would keep it safe. Before he could do this, he was killed. The day Mr. Foster was killed, Rick had collaborated with Jim to take one of the knives from the *Grimoire Danya* studio to get refurbished in Jim's gun shop. That was going to be his original alibi in case Mr. Foster started throwing out accusations of people breaking into his apartment; Rick and Jim would just claim they were both in the shop, which was in the neighborhood of Uptown, far from James Foster's home.

Rick drove to one of the side streets between Evanston and Roger's Park. From there, he went to the lake shore and carefully climbed over the rocks to the private beach of his grandfather's apartment building. The beach and parking lot didn't have security cameras - which was one of the reasons Mr. Foster was so adamant about having his own security system.

Since Rick had been building strength for his role as Dyllas, he could climb the beach's fence into the parking lot. He climbed the fire escape to James's apartment and then waited outside the window. Jim's men had been monitoring James's apartment long enough to see me coming and going with Jesse. They narrowed down the two-hour window in the evenings during which I usually came. Since there was no door between the living room and the kitchen, Rick could look through to the living room and keep watch for when I came in. He knew the alarm would be off while I was there, so he worked the window open and hid in the hall closet until James settled down unsuspectingly in his bedroom.

The safe was too well-hidden to find in the living room, so Rick had assumed that it was in one of the other rooms. In his rather clumsy and desperate search in the kitchen, he knocked over a wine glass that was sitting on the kitchen counter. His grandfather heard the shatter and opened the bedroom door to see Rick attempting to hide in the hall closet.

Because of Mr. Foster's cataracts and hearing loss, he didn't recognize Rick's face or voice and aimed his gun. In a panic, Rick rushed him with a random knife he brought with him from the back of the gun shop. He killed his grandfather by accident while trying to keep from being shot and freaked out, but he knew that if the evidence stayed there, they would still be caught, especially if the police found the drugs while investigating the murder. He kept searching, but he wasn't able to find the safe before I returned. He hid in the hallway closet and listened as I found Mr. Foster's body and called the police. When I left to go to the lobby, he climbed back out of the window and descended the fire escape back to the ground before going back to his car via the beach.

  He told Jim what happened. Jim was angry because now there was a chance that Mr. Foster's murder could be traced back to him. His first inclination was be to get rid of Rick to cover up a loose end, but Rick's death would be noticed by the *Grimoire Danya* community and the murder would point to Jim anyway. He just told Rick that he would take care of everything. At first, they planned to frame me, but Mr. Foster's call to me to request that I pick his package from the mailroom cleared my name because I wouldn't have had enough time to pick up the package after my walk and get back up to the apartment to kill him. When Jim and Rick found out that Mr. Foster had called me, they planned instead to set up the crime so that there wouldn't be enough evidence to identify a killer.

  But Rick had grown wary of Jim and thought his uncle would betray him like Jim had betrayed Mr. Foster. Rick planted the murder weapon so that the police would find it in the gun shop (it may have been cleaned, but it would still match the size and shape of the wound). When the police found the receipt for the missing *Grimoire Danya* knife, they would notice the murder weapon when they searched the place. That would finger Jim as the murderer. Afterwards, all he had to say was that Jim had tried to frame him by stealing the *Grimoire Danya* knife and planting it in the gun shop.

In the meantime, Marietta and Mark suspected that Jim tried to involve Rick in this operation, although they didn't know Rick had been the one to kill James. While they were upset, they were willing to protect Rick for the sake of their family. Marietta wanted Jim in prison for the murder and supplied Rick with an alibi, saying that he was visiting her with Mark that weekend; exactly what she had told me.

After Rick confessed all of this, he plead guilty to the murder after much pressure from his family, hoping he might get a lighter sentence. Jim, while acquitted from the murder charge, was not released since all of the information tying him to the drug ring was incontestable. With the erratic way Rick had been behaving lately, Mark said it was almost like Rick had been expecting Jim's plan to cover up Mr. Foster's murder to fall apart. Were it not for his interference, there was a chance he and Jim could have gotten away with their plot. All Rick had ever wanted was to keep his web show safe from the publicity that would have destroyed it.

Epilogue

I met with Mark sometime after he was released from the hospital after the fight. We were leaning against my car in the park near my apartment building, both of us looking out over the lake as the sun shimmered over the surface. He had bruises on his face and stitches for a long cut on his arm. He looked a little worse for wear, but I didn't mind. It was hard to think the scars were ugly when I knew he had gotten those injuries protecting me.

"I'm gonna be heading out of town soon, to get away from all the publicity. Mom's been pressing me into it," he said.

I gave a half smile. "I don't blame you. I can't imagine how the reporters must be hounding you right now."

He shuddered and chuckled. "Don't remind me. They were this close to breaking into the studio the other day. They all wanted to get shots of sets for the last scene we ever filmed."

We fell into a comfortable silence. He tried to stretch and put his hands behind his head, but wound up wincing when his arm protested.

"Careful," I said. "You should take it easy. You're not Averad!"

I had meant it to be a joke, but the look on Mark's face was more sad than happy. "Yeah. I'm not Averad. I guess I'll never be him again."

I looked away, ashamed. "I'm sorry. I shouldn't have said that."

"Nah, it's alright. We had a good run. He was fun. A bastard, but a fun bastard," he said.

"Are you going to finish the last few shows? The ones you have footage for, anyway," I said.

Mark shrugged. "I don't know if people would watch them. Scandals like this spell doom for shows. Do you think the fans would want to see a convicted murderer as the hero?"

I clutched at my arms. "You're probably right..."

"Don't worry about it. I might not be in that role anymore, but once this has blown over a bit, I might audition for something else. Just because *Grimoire Danya* is over, doesn't mean I have to stop acting," Mark said.

"Is that your dream? To become a famous actor?" I asked.

"Well, I've got the famous part under my belt, now I just have to work more on the 'actor' bit," he said, with a laugh. It felt good to hear it and I joined him. "What about you? Are you going to stay in Chicago?"

"I think so," I said. "There will always be dogs to walk and houses to sit for."

"I hope those dogs of yours appreciate the person walking them," he said. "You're one of a kind, you know that?"

I felt my face heat up and knew, with embarrassment, that I would be beet-red. "Well...um, maybe."

Mark smiled at me. "No, seriously. I don't think I would have been able to keep my cool through all this if I was in your place."

"Thanks," I mumbled.

"Actually, if you're still around when I come back to the city, do you think we could catch dinner sometime?" he asked. He said it hopefully and I could only imagine the expression that must be on his face with the way my eyes were glued to the ground. Now was not the time to be shy. With a deep breath, I forced myself to look up at him and smile. "Yeah, I would really like that."

His smile was the most brilliant I had seen out of him yet. When I related the entire scene to Jennifer later on, she asked if it was at that point when he took me into a sweeping kiss. The answer was no, but I only answered with a shrug, just to keep her on her toes for a bit longer.

I was still curious as to how the drugs had been exchanged so secretly alongside the silver cylinders. After some more investigation, Neal and Carl were able to uncover how the drugs were being passed off during the deals – in the poop bags. The deals were commonly held in dog parks. What was the least suspicious object that a person could be holding in a dog park? A poop bag. No one would question why a person was holding a bag and absolutely no one would bother to look inside. It was the perfect method of exchange.

In the middle of all the media attention, Jennifer and I watched as the *Grimoire Danya* fandom imploded. Half of them were screaming that their hero was innocent while the other half were condemning Rick for his actions. Neither of us could bear to watch the show again after everything was over and we wanted to sell our DVD's. To my surprise, the scandal actually made many people want to see the show more than ever. In a twisted way, Rick had found a way to promote his series.

The next Friday night was the most peaceful night I had in what felt like months. My parents and Toby came by to take me out to dinner and help me make my apartment even more secure with better locks for the doors and windows. Having them around really drove it home that I was safe again. This nightmare was over. Once they had gone back home, Jennifer and I crashed in the living room, pigging out on ice cream and doing whatever else we needed to detoxify our brains from the last couple of weeks. A dog show was on and Jesse was cuddled comfortably next to me, looking up at me with his soulful eyes, begging for a hand-out. I wasn't fooled; I recognized those eyes from the same picture I got from Mr. Foster's apartment. I just kissed his head and assured him that, while he wouldn't be getting any ice cream, he would still be getting a bacon treat later on. He wagged his tail happily. He knew he *was* a good boy.

Made in the USA
Monee, IL
04 February 2022